WORLD'S FARE

MICHAEL HUYCK

MACABRE Ink

"I travel a lot, son. A lot. And I know the look of another traveler, one like me. Where you headed?"

Darryl spun the fork in his mashed potatoes, mixing the gravy in.

"Eastbound, right?"

He spun slower. The man fed him, and there was a cost.

There was always a cost.

"New Orleans," Darryl said. "I'm going to New Orleans."

"What for?"

"Ghosts. I'm supposed to see the ghosts." He took a bite of the potatoes, hoping that was enough, but it was never enough.

"Lots of ghosts in New Orleans, I suspect. Almost infinite ghosts. It feels like a haunted city. What are you going to do, count them?"

Filling his mouth with a fat fork of meatloaf, Darryl chewed and thought, then shook his head. He waited until he could swallow, swallowed it with sweet tea, and gave up a little more. "We're looking for a particular one, but I don't know who. Sh'Nae didn't tell me."

"Sh'Nae?"

"She is my friend."

"Where is she?" the man stopped, then shook his head. He took his own bite of the meatloaf and chewed slowly. Carefully. When he finished, he started back up. "We should go find your friend, then. You haven't said as much, so please excuse me if I'm wrong, but I'm thinking you're not certain how you're getting to New Orleans."

Darryl's eyes lit up. "You're going there?"

CHAPTER ONE

Year: 2317
Location: Near Chicago, Illinois

"How'd you get him, Benet?" Dahlgren asked. He was standing in permanent judgment, as he always did, with his feet slightly apart and his arms crossed. Looman mimicked him.

"A ridiculous number of shifts spent tying down the split second he was shot. I went through a dozen patient agents before I found one who'd stick it all the way through. She's running this operation now. Name's Alex Donna."

"Never heard of her."

"You'll hear more. Much more. She's going places."

"What's next?"

"We're planting him, along with two deep volunteers, in early USA. The presentists are looking for him in likely places, but they're going to find him in one that's unlikely. That'll up their confidence. Then they go in after him, and we let them. Afterward, we follow."

"So, you're giving them what they want? Sounds dangerous and slow."

"It is dangerous, but not as dangerous as them getting him on their own. And does it matter if it's slow?"

"Not really. I guess. What about the deeps?"

"Usual story. Unhappy enough in their lives now that they're willing to take on new ones. They know that they're being reprogrammed, and they'll never be back. Neither one of them cares."

"That's convenient."

"It's frighteningly easy to find deep volunteers."

Dahlgren watched the low barge, its bow sporting rust flowers across its marine green paint, chug up onto a spit of sand. To the left a sagging dock hung onto a single motor launch with a frayed rope, and in the other direction the sand spit broke into rip rap that continued down the island's shore.

"Carry on," he said, then turned to head back into the Titor Center. Looman followed.

———————

Parked at the head of the spit were three small, battery-operated utility vehicles, each pulling a long and simple trailer with small rubber tires and a bed made of oxidized tin. When the barge land ed, a crewman at the front pulled two pins, one on each side of the front, then jacked a simple handle along the barge's port side near the bow. He looked to make sure everyone was clear, then pulled the handle and dropped the bow onto the sand.

Drivers, each in tan coveralls, exited their utility vehicles and walked down to the barge, with the first one there picking up the handle at the front of a coffinlike box mounted on wheels. He squeezed a lever on the handle and the box pushed forward with an electric whir. As the man directed the box toward one of the trailers, the next man went into the barge, selected a box, and re peated the process. By the time the last man had his box up to the trailer, the first man had winched his box onto a trailer behind the utility vehicle. When he had it seated, with two straps pulled tight, he walked the empty trailer back down to the barge and parked it. This was repeated two more times while the barge crew hoisted its bow and made to pull out. The utility vehicle left down a single wide asphalt strip to the Titor Center, pulling through a double-ended driveway to back up to the loading dock. There the process was reversed.

Doctor Finley didn't arrive until the boxes were unloaded in the Feynman Laboratory, their seals cracked and the contents observable. Two of them were the agents he'd prepared for this mission, agents who now carried new histories and went by new names, but what those were Finley didn't know. It was all part of security compartmentalization, and only the project's lead knew every piece. One of the agents was also a guest, and that was a first for Finley. He'd seen guests come through the Titor Center before, but never one who was a NUSA agent. He was amazed that such a thing existed.

The third box held a mystery, another guest whose sole preparation included erasing his memory. That was it. He wasn't provided with anything new to build on, a technique which used to apply to criminals but fell out of favor. The brain had a way of back filling voids, but its methods were unpredictable. Mostly what it left was the equivalent of static, and what good was that going forward? Finley shook his head and continued his examination.

"Are the escorts ready?" he asked. The nurse with him nodded and waved a group in from a viewing room. There were six in all, two to go with each of the travelers. They were dressed in period clothing, blue jeans and flannel shirts and boots, a fashion that had fallen away at least a century before, but it still looked comfortable and warm to Finley. Each one wore a pouch on their hip, a pouch which Finley knew carried their impulse director. Just in case.

The six broke up on their own, with two beside each box, while Finley briefed them. "We'll be using an optical replicator, transmitting images that they'll see as I pull them out of anesthesia. They've been patterned to follow the images, and at a given point each will shift. When you see them shift, you follow using them as an anchor. Does anyone here need suggestion?"

Two of the agents motioned, and the nurse came over with a blister pack, popping out one small, white pill into their hands. The nurse then gave each of the six a still-sealed blister pack, which were then tucked into pants pockets.

Finley reached in and tapped the face piece on the guest agent. "Everyone here knows to take the viewer off before shifting back, right? And bring it with you. These things are expensive." Finley knew he probably didn't need to say that, but it'd happened before. Agents really didn't give a rat's ass about the center's equipment. "Okay. We're going into the observation room. Good luck."

CHAPTER TWO

Year: 2010
Location: San Pedro, California

Milk sucked, and it didn't matter if they squeezed it from cows or almonds. Darryl dropped the spoon into his cereal bowl, hungry but exasperated. Looking around the kitchen, at the black microwave hovering over the black range with the shiny glass top, he decided he couldn't work either. Instead, he walked his breakfast over to the sink and dropped it full onto the dishes below. Something shattered, but he didn't look. Instead, he walked back to the living room. His head was beginning to hum. He paused, hoping to wait it out. There wasn't any risk here, no pressure or unknowns, and there certainly weren't any of the dead. That much he knew for certain. He'd walked its rooms and halls for three years now and there'd not been one once. Not in the closets and not behind the toilet. Nowhere. But somehow, that made it worse. When Sh'Nae asked why, he couldn't explain.

He wished she would come home.

Darryl found himself at the end of the love seat and staring at the closest cushion. It was tan, with raised rows in the cloth. There was a name for that. He remembered hearing it once about a pair of pants he wore. And the cushion, he could sit there. It was an option. Next to it was the couch, same cloth, with an extra bank of cushions tempting him to lie down. Farther to the right was the recliner with its soft blue fabric smelling of things soft. It had a magic wooden handle which made it longer and more comfortable, and Darryl loved the recliner. The recliner was closest to the remote control, but he didn't know how to work that, either. Sh'Nae worked everything associated with electricity.

Moving past the living room options, he went to the hallway where Sh'Nae hung pictures of people Darryl didn't know. This could work, too. He could stand here. Or he could sit on the countertop in the kitchen. Of course, there was the bathroom. He could shower again.

That's where he was standing and thinking when Sh'Nae walked in that afternoon. She was carrying a take-and-bake pizza and a bottle of Dr. Pepper, which for Darryl was a celebratory drink. He looked up at her and tried to smile, but it hurt. She saw his efforts and flashed her bright smile back. She always had that smile at the ready.

"You can hear it?" she asked. Darryl nodded, but with enthusiasm. The hum laid the foundation of his afternoon, but it was fading now.

Sh'Nae changed the subject. "Ganns and I had lunch; he has a new project for us."

It's something special, Darryl thought.

"It's something special, I think."

Darryl nodded. "It's time," he said, and it was. It'd been a year since their last one. "Where are we going?" He found it a relief, because the apartment was becoming too much. Even sitting on the balcony and staring out at Catalina Island couldn't keep all the rough edges tucked in anymore.

"New Orleans."

Darryl's face darkened. That was the place that had the hurricane. "Katrina?"

"Oh no, too new for Ganns. You know that. It's the Robert Charles riots. More specifically, he wants us to find Robert Charles."

After three hours of standing still, Darryl found the energy for three steps to the love seat. "I don't know anything about Robert Charles." While it was true, it was also a distraction. Darryl read, and he read a lot. It was apparent some cities had more for him to see, more death history, and he imagined New Orleans would be up there near New

York, San Francisco, and Galveston, all places he dreaded and refused to know. Ganns knew about them, but Darryl hadn't ever refused New Orleans. Now he wished he'd had.

"There are only two places he wants us to visit, the place where it started and the place where it ended. The middle, it's…"

"…repeatable." Darryl ended the sentence in one of Ganns' favorite terms. His position was that history was a short movie on infinite replay. Change the names and change the countries and it just all goes on again. "When?"

"The day after tomorrow." She paused. "We still have our show at the Grand tomorrow. I bought you a new shirt, a black one, like you asked for."

Darryl dropped his stare to his knees.

"The tie is black too, but with a pattern. And a gold tie chain."

Darryl didn't move.

"They're on the table, if you want to look. I'm going to sit on the balcony and read, okay?"

Sh'Nae picked up her book and went out, sliding the glass door shut quietly, while Darryl sat. He blinked, slowly, and letting it all run off of him. He couldn't think about it now, but he couldn't not think about it now. When he recovered his voice, Darryl whispered "but I don't want to go to the Grand." When no one answered, he added "I like tie chains."

The next evening found Darryl in his shirt, tie, and tie chain, staring at the bathroom mirror. Both he and Sh'Nae were ready and waiting when Ganns arrived, fifteen minutes late, his pressed lip smile about as broad as it ever got. He touched Sh'Nae on the cheek as he walked in and past her to Darryl. "You're looking good, Darryl."

"I don't want to do this," Darryl said.

"You never want to do this, but we'll follow my rules, right?"

Ganns stood there, short and stocky and hard, a ring of dark hair around his bald crown and thin eyes peering. Darryl thought he looked like some comedian he'd seen on television. "They work."

"Sure. Your rules."

"I ask the questions of you, just like we've rehearsed. You answer it, any way you want, and I move on. The audience gets to ask me questions, but not you. You just sit and look over their heads. Focus on a spot on the wall. If you don't like the question, don't answer. I'll fix it."

"Is there a spot?" Darryl asked. What he wanted to say was *that doesn't always work.*

"There's always a spot. If anyone gets pushy, we stop and escort them to the door. I've done it before, right?"

Darryl nodded. Ganns had. Some of these shows were okay, and some were good. None had really been bad. Not too bad. Just before the show it was bad.

"So, you guys ready?" Ganns turned to Sh'Nae. "You set to go?" He had his keys out and Darryl saw the BMW key chain he'd given Ganns for his birthday last year. Ganns tended to rub it when he was distracted, which wasn't now.

Sh'Nae smiled and waved at the door. "You got this, Darryl," he said, and he walked back out. He'd been in their apartment for all of a minute. As they walked down the hallway, Sh'Nae asked questions about their trip to New Orleans, and Darryl listened. Ganns himself would be driving, and that was good. They'd sleep in Tucson, El Paso, San Antonio, Houston, and when they arrived in New Orleans there was a hotel with a big clock that was THE place to be if a hurricane came. Darryl liked hearing this, and it lifted his spirits. There'd be death at the other end, but there was death everywhere. At least this time death would come with étouffée.

They'd done other shows at the Grand and he'd been there plenty of times besides. When he had time, he liked to stare at the decorations on the walls straddling the stage. Once they remained until the building was emptied of customers and, with Sh'Nae watching carefully from the stage, he tried sitting on the balcony once, but he couldn't see from the back and the front was just too high off of the ground. This time he'd stay on the stage, staring out at the faces.

Darryl pushed that vision away.

They parked behind the theater and, with a quick phone call from Ganns, were ushered into the back door. Sh'Nae took Darryl's hand and led him, so he kept his face down and his eyes mostly closed. During the walk in he mostly watched the shine off his black leather shoe tips, but he had to look up when they turned into their dressing room, which wasn't much more than a closet. There was a freestanding wardrobe, a desk, and a small mirror hung on the wall above it. On the wall to the left was a rat ty love seat.

"Take a sit," Ganns said, pointing at the love seat, "and I'll find Lindsey. I can hear the murmur out there." He paused, his eyes flicking quickly to Sh'Nae and back to Darryl. "We're on in just a few, okay?" He gave Darryl's right shoulder a squeeze and walked back out of the room.

Sitting on the couch, Darryl started whispering to himself. At first it was inaudible, just sitting on his hands with his neck bent down slightly. His eyes were open, but not focused, and that meant she was losing him. He needed redirection. Sh'Nae sat down and said "Rapper's Delight." Darryl nodded and repeated it after her. "Rapper's Delight. 1979." Sh'Nae waited.

"The Breaks," 1980. "Jazzy Sensation," 1981. "The Message," 1982. "Sucker M.C.'s," 1983. "Friends," 1984."

She set one hand on his.

"La Di Da Di," 1985, "6 in the Mornin'," 1986. "Paid in Full," 1987."

"Great raps," Sh'Nae said.

"Straight Outta Compton," 1988. "Fight the Power," 1989."

She had to hurry. They didn't have much time to get through the routine, and this routine could be long. "Bonita Applebum," 1990" she added. Darryl sped up.

"Mind Playing Tricks on Me," 1991. "Nuthin' but a 'G' Thang," 1992. "C.R.E.A.M," 1993. "Juicy," 1994. "Dear Mama," 1995. "California Love," 1996.

"Wait," Sh'Nae whispered. She leaned in close to Darryl. "Serrano, right?" She said it slowly, like reading from a script for the first time.

"Serrano." He paused, thinking. "Serrano Huasteco". He pronounced the latter word *hooasteeco*, which made Sh'Nae smile.

"Halabi. Chili Wili. Aleppo. Tears of Fire." It was going well, but would Ganns wait? He had to.

"Tianying. Gambia. Stumpy." He was close to the point where Sh'Nae could interject. She leaned in, and he flinched. "Takanotsume. Shipkas. Royal black. Pimenta de Bode. Peter Pepper."

That was her doorway, a doorway she spent the better part of a year figuring out.

"Peter Piper?" she asked. "Peter...pepper," he repeated, slowly. "Peter Piper?"

"Peter..." Darryl said, then he nodded. He smiled his worn-out smile, because the lists, as much as they helped, took something from him. "Let's do this." He stood up and walked toward the door and stepped out. The space there couldn't be called a hallway, because hallways have walls. It was more of an empty space riddled with fans, partitions, pulleys, and mops. Ganns was coming their way, motioning for them to follow, then he turned on his heels. They wove in and out of the obstacles to the right end, turned around the back curtain, and walked up to the center of the front. On the other side the buzz of voices, muffled as it was by hundreds of pounds of curtain in front of them, was loud. Ganns knew better than to hesitate. He walked up to the part between the curtains and held it open, allowing Darryl, then Sh'Nae, to pass through. The audience broke into polite applause.

There was a table set up to the right and, in the center, a podium. Darryl and Sh'Nae took the two closest chairs at the table, with Sh'Nae thumping her microphone and then Darryl's after they sat. Ganns waited at the podium until they were situated and the applause faded, then he began.

"Good evening, ladies and gentlemen, and thank you for coming. You just finished watching our latest offering from Second Sight Pictures. I won't ask if you enjoyed it, because enjoyment is not our goal at Second Sight. What I will ask you is if you'll ever forget it."

At this the audience broke into emphatic applause. Darryl stared at them, not at individuals, but at the whole group. He saw it as one thing, one living thing with hundreds of eyes and hands, responding to the verbal prods Ganns let slip so simply from his lips. Darryl also wondered at the applause. Who first thought that beating their hands together signified satisfaction? How did that person get others to join in?

"It's odd to think that this, our crowning achievement, was born of failure." Here came the back story Ganns always provided. He thought it helped connect the audience to the film. "It began when I provided Darryl an artifact, a shell from World War II, and sent him and Sh'Nae off to Okinawa." Ganns continued on with his spiel for another ten minutes before he opened Darryl up for questioning, so Darryl did what came naturally, he searched for the dead. They were almost always there.

There was only one this time, an accomplishment considering how old the theater looked. She was an older lady slumped in her seat hard, seven rows back, near the end to Darryl's right. Her head tilted to one shoulder, revealing only her closed eyes and the bridge of her nose, and she wore a bag of a dress with a floral pattern and no collar. The buttons were simple and white, and the pattern was faded. Darryl guessed her to be from the 1940s, but there was no telling with old people. They all looked the same dead. Darryl scanned to room, seeing a smattering of empty chairs. It wasn't weird that the seats on either side were filled with real people but hers wasn't. Not really. But he still wondered. If he went there, if he sat on her, could he feel her? In all his years, he'd never tried. He didn't touch them, and he didn't talk to them. He didn't want any more from their world than he already had.

The live faces he saw were kind, at least most of them. People who came to Ganns' shows were usually in the forties or older, and the blue hairs were out in force tonight in San Pedro. It wasn't fair to call them blue hairs, because that crowd was predominantly white women. This audience was mixed, busting out with blue, white, gray, stained black, and unnatural red locks. Darryl was searching for the obvious toupee when he felt a hand on his shoulder. It was Sh'Nae's sign that he needed to rejoin them. A hand on the shoulder meant talk and one on the back meant stop talking.

"When you arrived, you were provided a flier with a set of ground rules and their basis, but they bear repeating. First—you ask your question to me and not to Darryl. Second—I will decide if Darryl will answer the question, not you. Third—if you do not comply with numbers one and two, you will be escorted from the room. There are no exceptions and no refunds." At this point six large men entered from the rear of the room, three on each side. They stood in the walkways, faces congenial but their bulk imposing. Ganns continued. "And with that, we're open for questions." Several hands shot up.

They'd done the routine multiple times for each of their three movies together, and Darryl still had no idea how Ganns chose who would be answered and who wouldn't. Sometimes five hands went in the air, sometimes ten, but that didn't matter. What mattered was that there'd be five questions and there were always more than five to be asked. There were tens, hundreds, maybe it was infinite. But only five would be asked and maybe five would be answered, depending on if the questioners followed the rules.

The first question was a standard one. "Have you ever seen the ghost of anyone you knew?" Ganns had a theory why everyone asked this. He said they wanted confirmation that they would get a chance to again see someone they once knew. That there was something orderly and fine about the hereafter. But Darryl's answer wouldn't help them. The first time it was asked he just said "no", because no was the truth. That night Ganns nursed a different answer from him, one just as honest but more complex. He asked Darryl a few questions, like why and why not and how do you know? Questions that made Darryl think past the flickering images staining every day of his life. Perhaps Ganns the showman needed a bit of drama, but Darryl didn't think so. Though he didn't really know Ganns (he suspected no one really knew Ganns), he trusted that he'd do one thing consistently. He'd do right by his audience. He'd give them their money's worth. That was what made Ganns, a man who never once needed to work, a hardworking man, nonetheless.

Darryl replied with the canned answer. He knew all the words and the order they came in.

"I don't think so, but I'm not sure. They are hazy, these ghosts." This much was true, though he was certain if he saw Sh'Nae as a ghost he'd know her. Before, there wasn't anyone to know.

Ganns smiled down on Darryl from the podium, then pointed high in the air. Darryl looked up to the balcony. "You. Young man in the red striped shirt." The teenager stood up.

"You mentioned in the movie that the shell you carried came from Arisaka. Do you know which kind?" Darryl immediately recognized this as a test, because the lines he spoke through the move were very specific. He opened his mouth to answer, but Ganns interrupted. "I don't think this is necessary."

"It's okay," Darryl said. "Okay. What I said, sir," he thought for a second, trying to recover the words. It was there in his memory. Everything was. "What I said was that I sloshed through the lapping waters to dry sand, then went in another four meters and dropped to my knees. From my pocket I withdrew the rifle shell. A 7.7 and, from what I was told, most likely shot from an Arisaka Type 99, one of the rare sniper variants. "That's what I said in the movie, a 7.7 from an Arisaka Type 99 of the sniper variant."

"Do you know how rare?" the teenager asked.

"No idea. I don't like guns." This seemed manageable at first, but the questions were wandering off script. The buzzing began in Darryl's brain, but he pushed it off. "They kill people."

"So do cars," the teenager said. He raised his hand in emphasis, but he was shut down.

"You're done," Ganns said. He pointed at the sound man at the back of the room, making a slashing motion, and the boy's microphone was cut off. "I'll remind you, each of you, that this isn't a free-for-all. You get one question, and that question cannot undermine Mr. Green. I won't put up with it. With his skills come special sensitivities, and I won't have them abused. Who's next?" The pause that came after was long, too long, When Darryl couldn't list, he found counting in his head worked as a cheap re placement.

One thousand. Nine hundred and ninety-nine. Nine hundred and ninety-eight. Nine hundred and ninety-seven. Nine hundred and ninety-six.

He felt a hand on his shoulder.

This one was an older man, a much older man. He smiled at Darryl, shining his personal light at the stage. Immediately Darryl liked him.

"I was at Okinawa in the spring of '45 with the 22nd Marines." He paused, looking down for a moment. "And I remember that beach clearly. I've been back twice since then, and one thing which struck me is how the beach has changed. I was wondering, when you see the ghosts, do you see them where they died, or where you are now?

As the question brought focus, the buzz dialed down. Darryl nodded his head, listening the way Sh'Nae taught him to. When he was certain the man was finished, he cleared his throat.

"It's as things are when I'm there. I cannot see the past, their time. For example, when in Okinawa, surrounded by the sounds and smells of the battle and the men, all the men, I still saw the boat Sh'Nae and I came to the beach on, too. I saw its living crew." There were several hands up in the air as he answered, and that was a good thing. The quicker they asked the quicker he finished, and the quicker they could return to their apartment. Maybe they could pack tonight.

The man Ganns chose was a tall fellow, and gaunt. His chin and nose were competing crags and the flat top he wore his hair in did nothing to diminish his angularity. Everything from his brown slacks to his blue shirt to the way his arms fidgeted autonomously screamed of discomfort, and Darryl felt it. The buzzing grew louder, it swelled.

The man pulled a pocket watch from his pants and looked at it, eliciting a sigh from Ganns that everyone enjoyed via his micro phone. "I have this theory. The theory is that you can tell plenty about a man only by looking at his roots. Like a tall tree, strong roots are necessary to stay upright. To gather water. To suffer fire."

"Do you have a question, sir?" Ganns asked, bearing his impatience.

"I do. You are a very interesting man, Mr. Green. I'm interested in your roots. Can you tell us something about your past, before you began working with Mr. Ganns? Anything at all, please." The gentleman gently folded his arms.

Darryl knew he couldn't. He looked up to find Ganns staring down, and the buzzing waxed. First it was with the freeway feeling, like it always did. Darryl hadn't explained this to many people, but he had to Sh'Nae. He told her when it comes on it's like there's an L.A. freeway cloverleaf centered around, and passing through, his skull. There's constant traffic from all directions heading in all directions. The feeling isn't painful, but it is captivating. Like all the world's knowledge revealed, but he has to read it all, and all right now. He slumped; his face aimed at the first row of the auditorium instead of where the man stood. The buzzing filled his ears and left his cheeks numb. He never felt Sh'Nae's hand on his right shoulder or Ganns' on his left. The night was nothing but droning now.

Ganns flicked the left turn signal and changed lanes, avoiding SR86 and still chewing his lower lip. He hadn't said a word since before Palm Springs, and that was fine with Sh'Nae. When he grew petulant, silence was golden.

She chided herself, because he wasn't petulant. Not really. He just wasn't learning Darryl, how he worked and what set him off. For Ganns, last night was a matter of embarrassment, but for Darryl it hurt. It physically hurt. Sh'Nae didn't know how or how much, but she knew when he was in pain. The proof was in Darryl's follow-up. He'd been mostly sleeping for the last fifteen hours, waking only to struggle to the back seat of Ganns' car.

That said, he seemed upbeat about the trip to New Orleans. For some reason, regardless of the weight it left on his soul, Sh'Nae found Darryl's second sight comforted him. He was in his element then, at his most rational. More than rational, he was almost like a normal guy, and Darryl was rarely normal.

She sat back and watched the desert go by. Besides the faded ribbon of highway before them, it was flat and tan, broken by scrub and rocks and occasionally sharp plants jutting into the sky. Where Sh'Nae liked

L.A., the harbor lights, and the hilly streets of San Pedro, the desert surrounding the city of angels was depressing. She'd be raised in Corinth, Mississippi, a tree covered land of slow days and thick air. Alabama and Mississippi were both close enough to drop in for lunch (where she could get a proper slug burger instead of just Tommy's), but back then she never saw why she'd want to even drive that far. If she needed exotica, she could take the bus to Memphis.

Slipping off her sandals, she put her feet up on the dashboard. It was the only time Ganns hated when she put her feet up. Stop, she told herself. Just stop it. She decided to break the silence.

"I Googled Robert Charles last night." She turned to watch his reaction. He bobbed his head, relaxing his neck. That was a good start.

"What did you think?"

"It's complicated."

"Most riots are. Open my satchel," he said, patting the leather bag he carried with him everywhere. He continued while she did. "The riots are one story, from the way racism swings to the way race relations in New Orleans always differed from the rest of the south, but it's Robert's short stay in New Orleans that intrigues me most."

Sh'Nae took a garish red book from the satchel. "CARNIVAL OF FURY—is it any good?"

"I don't know if history is ever good or bad, it just is. The author tries to build his story on facts, but he surmises quite a bit. I suspect there were other academics who would hold Dr. Hair to task for that." This was standard Ganns speak. "Would you like it? I think so. They portray Robert Charles as complicated, which fits your assessment."

"Do you think so?" This wasn't the way to go to keep the peace, but she couldn't help herself. No, she wouldn't help herself.

"Think what?"

"That he was complicated?"

"I don't think anyone alive will ever know. It may be that inciting a riot was exactly what he wanted, which would certainly make him complicated. It may also be that he thought no deeper than his own anger, which wouldn't." He tapped the wheel a couple times, then added "Or maybe he was responding to fear. I'd love to ask him."

"Is that why we're going there? To figure out his motivation?" He nodded as Sh'Nae asked it, but she already knew the answer. Ganns wanted his documentaries to be one thing above all else, and that was revelatory. If there wasn't a tarp he could pull back for the audience, it didn't interest him. That was why their trip to Okinawa didn't focus on the battle, but instead on the people dying. Ganns thought the American public needed to not just know that heroism is bloody, he wanted them to see it. To face it. That was why she had the respect for him she did.

So there. The conversation worked. He was unwound and Sh'Nae didn't have to say a single thing about what she really thought. When she said "it's complicated" she meant it, but not in the way Ganns knew, or ever could know.

They were past Phoenix and just shy of Guadalupe when Darryl sat up. He waggled his nose and looked out both side windows, then slumped back. "Are we there yet?" Sh'Nae couldn't tell if he was being serious, and she wasn't sure he knew himself. For Darryl, adulting came in flashes of sarcasm, cynicism, and exploration buried between folds of wonderfully simple naivete. Most of the time little answers to his little questions were enough and she loved him for that, but when he did this, when he whispered irony, she loved him even more.

She couldn't play along, though. That would ruin it for him. "Not yet," she said, "but close." He didn't respond, and she didn't look, but she suspected he wore a little smile.

They continued, Ganns with one hand dangling at the bottom of the steering wheel and his eyes locked on the horizon, stopping only to gas up north of Arizona City. There Sh'Nae picked up two pepperoni sticks and one kippered beef stick, along with three sodas, for the final leg. No one looked particularly tired now, but the desert was long, low, and hot. No one needed to fade.

When they stopped at the Omni and parked, Sh'Nae ushered Darryl out and took their overnight bags out of the trunk while Ganns checked them in. He was a stickler about the way they traveled, about restroom stops and hotel choices and packing travel bags separate from their big suitcases. Not that Sh'Nae or Darryl brought a big suitcase, only Ganns did. He could follow his own rules if he wanted to.

The hotel was a beautiful place sprawling in the Tucson heat, with brick and pale stucco and, on the far side, splashes of golf course in the deepest green broken up by expanses of brown earth. No one looked further that way, because they didn't golf. Ganns took his bag and went into his room while Sh'Nae led Darryl into theirs. He dropped both of their bags on the floor inside, looked around, then chose the farthest bed to sprawl on. This was consistent, as he'd be out most of the day after one of his fugues. She was surprised he was awake as long as he was.

After he was out, she pulled off his shoes and placed them at the foot of the bed for him to find should he wake up, then she dug through her bag to find her book, her one piece, and her cover-up. She changed, grabbed the key card and a towel, and headed for the pool. Other than an old man who's wrinkled flesh spoke of decades spent sunning, the deck was clear. Sh'Nae suspected that the heat had something to do with it but decided she didn't care. It wasn't anything like a Mississippi summertime.

After a quick dip to cool her skin, she cracked the spine of THE UNVANQUISHED, a favorite she'd read at least annually since she'd graduated college ten years previous. The novel felt like her heart, at once conflicted and resolute. It was southern, it was honest, and it was confusing. The way it ended, with the verbena and its inherent illusion of health, put a perfect bow on the story. She'd just read about moving the trunk when Ganns' shadow crossed over.

"How's Ringo?" he asked, spreading his towel on the lounge next to hers. "Any new developments?"

"You're a shit," she replied, smiling. It was different when it was just the two of them, no Darryl there to watch over, or Darryl there just watching. "I almost knocked on your door when I walked by, you know."

He nodded. "I'm glad you didn't, to be honest. I'm too tired right now to impress a young beauty like you."

"No need for that, old man. Just lay there and I'll impress myself."

"Who you calling old?" He lowered his glasses on the bridge of his nose imperiously, and Sh'Nae responded by pointing at him.

They spent the afternoon that way, intermittently cooling in the water, heating in the sun, and generally alone in the presence of each other. That was their signature dynamic.

Darryl was still asleep when Sh'Nae came back to the room, his shoes exactly where she'd placed them when she'd left for the pool. He'd sunk into the mattress, his relaxation displaying that he was healing. At least until the next time. She showered, dressed in her long cotton pajamas (she had to keep the room cool, too cool, for Darryl's sake), and by eight, at the beginning of the skirmish with Sartoris, she set the novel aside and let the travel day catch up with her.

The trip between Tucson and El Paso was one long yawn. Not even a long one, as from hotel door to hotel door it was less than six hours, but there was no explaining the way Ganns traveled. Sh'Nae suspected that he framed his decisions, and therefore himself, as necessarily enigmatic. She also suspected that they were enigmatic solely for the sake of eccentricity. He said he was a Hollywood boy, born and raised. How could he not be?

They chatted about nothing for the duration and the trip left her empty, unlike the ones where they bantered or even argued. There was satisfaction in those, somewhere. This time they talked about the colors on new cars, or how semis seemed to have more axles today than they used to have. The road itself was miserable, just vast expanses of dirt, rock, and scrub. Sh'Nae found herself wondering why anyone had ever come to the southwest. What drew them? There were fences and cattle, which meant the wide-open spaces were a cheap way for cattlemen to make money, but where did they get the water? If she really cared, it'd all be very confusing. But she didn't. She was just bored.

Without a fugue to recover from, Darryl was twitching in the back seat. Early on he'd taken to playing the license plate game, but after he had over twenty California plates and not a single Idaho, he fell into mumbling and gave up. Since then, he'd been repeating lists beneath his breath and that'd mostly worked. Mostly. Kicking the back of

Sh'Nae's seat helped him the rest of the way, and she took it. She always took it.

Apparently, there wasn't a resort to stay at in El Paso, because they wandered off I-10 to a Marriott, which was Ganns' backup travel destination. Once again, they checked in.

When the door clicked shut, Darryl thought about rolling over, about sitting up, but it wasn't time yet. He needed to work the day over. Not the entire day, because it was mostly variations on the license plate game, but just the end.

After he'd flopped on his bed, still completely dressed, Sh'Nae waited a few minutes and then changed into her swimsuit, like she almost always did, and left the room with a book in hand. He watched her change, eyes barely open and his vision fuzzy through his eyelashes. When he did this, which was every chance he got, something about the stripping of her jeans and sliding on of her two-piece left a burning at the bottom of his belly. She was neither tall nor short, but she was perfectly proportionate, and her skin was like a shallow cup of coffee. Her hair was a coiled bed of springs, thick and bouncy. The funny thing was that, when he saw her, all of her, he only remembered her deep, black eyes. While he wanted to do something, to say something, he never did. Instead, he always pretended to sleep, because he knew she'd never knowingly let him watch. If she caught him, she'd never change there again.

Darryl kept his mouth shut.

The difference this time wasn't that she changed, or that she left with a book, it was what she said in the lobby before they came up to their room. That's what had him thinking.

There'd been sharp words between Sh'Nae and Ganns after they pulled into El Paso, but Darryl didn't know what about. They were on a broad street, with lots of cars and businesses, and at one light there were two bodies slumped against a light pole. From their clothes, Darryl didn't think they'd died too long ago, perhaps only in the last twenty years, but he couldn't be sure. He remembered when he looked like them, with dirty hair and ragged layers of shirts. One was barefoot and the other had no laces in his floppy and torn tennis shoes.

"…not a cause. Every time, every time. Can't we choose a story for the sake of the story?" Sh'Nae had asked Ganns. Darryl didn't know what that meant. They were stopped at the light, and the bodies were one lane over. That lane was empty, leaving maybe ten feet of empty space between Darryl's window and the dead woman's open eyes. They were solid white.

"I didn't get into this for entertainment. I developed my production company specifically to tell stories which need to be told." When Ganns' voice went low and quiet, that meant he was stressed, and when Ganns was stressed, everyone got stressed.

Darryl chose to stare at the dead man's face, instead.

His eyes were closed, but his mouth was slack, his lips smeared with bits of white. The both of them could have died in their sleep, and they probably had. Their legs were straight out in front of them on the sidewalk. Maybe it was cold the night they died? Maybe they froze? There wasn't any blood, and no damage. Their clothes, filthy and tattered, were still straight.

"…remarkable stories, yes. All of them great, but do you need to include oppression and guilt in everything?" They were driving now, and the distraction was left behind them. Darryl kept searching the street. There'd be more. Somewhere.

"Guilt?" Darryl saw Ganns turn his head away from the wind shield for a second to look at Sh'Nae. "Guilt?"

She nodded. "Yes, guilt. Look, I know you hate it."

"For a damn good reason. Okinawa had nothing to do with white guilt."

"Didn't it? What about the internment segment? And what are we doing now? I read this last night." She shook a red book at Ganns. "Good learning, but it's still just feeding your white guilt. This whole trip will be. It gets old, Ganns."

"Why? It's real."

"I get that, but when it's always there, when it's a portion of your every thought, it loses sincerity. That's all there is to it. I can't believe you're always in your hair shirt. It doesn't make sense, okay? Not for anyone."

21

Darryl kept staring out the window, hoping for more bodies.

There was a pause, a very long pause, then Ganns finally nodded. "Let's talk about it more when we get a room?" When she answered, Sh'Nae's voice changed. She sounded happier. "Sure. Let's do that."

Darryl stopped staring out the window and looking for more corpses, and instead stared at the back of Sh'Nae's head. He'd heard that tone before and he wondered what it meant, because it meant something. It wasn't a normal tone, not one she'd ever used with him. Not one he'd heard with anyone besides Ganns. That it wasn't normal was all he knew, and that's what stuck in his brain as he lay on the bed.

There were four doors in their motel room, if you could count the sliding kind on the closet. Besides it, there was the bathroom door, the front door, and the one on the wall next to the dresser holding the television. He stared at the television, with its black screen and remote control with probably fifty but tons.

Getting up, Darryl picked up the remote and counted the buttons. There were forty-one.

The other door, the one through the wall, that was the one Sh'Nae had gone through. He stared at it for several seconds, trying to see something different, some reason why she'd chosen it. The closet and bathroom, she hadn't gone there in her swimsuit. That much made sense, but the two remaining would probably lead to the pool. Somehow. But the front door had a little brass thing in the middle, something Darryl could stare out of when there were noises in the hallway. The fourth door, it didn't. Even its doorknob looked different, though they both had twisting locks on them. Darryl checked the unnamed door, turning the knob slowly, and found he could open it.

On the far side he found another door, one which butted right up with his own, and instead of having a doorknob it had a flat and round brass plate. It was cracked, just slightly, and beyond Darryl heard voices. Voices he didn't recognize, at least not at first. He leaned in closer and pushed the door open a bit farther. One of them was male, but that was all Darryl could tell. He wasn't saying words, but instead he filled the air with whispers and gasps. The other, the other one he knew. It was Sh'Nae.

22

She spoke low, her voice husky and random. Instead of speaking in sentences, she spat words as if they stung her lips. Like the man, Sh'Nae made noises, too. Small groans and deep breaths. There was something else, like the sound made when he dried himself off with the towel. It was repetitive. It quickened. He leaned closer to the door, listening, sniffing. Then two things happened almost at once. Almost.

At first Darryl knew what he was hearing. Back when he lived on the street, when he slept beneath an overpass where the Harbor Freeway merged with Gaffey, he'd seen sex. They'd meet up there, sometimes, to zip together sleeping bags for a muffled bit of joy. Some just humped on the concrete, one hand on the chain link fence beside them to keep from rolling down the slope to the street below. Humping and sex was all Darryl knew it as, really. That and the words and the sounds that went with it. The look, like there was wrestling beneath the blanket, he knew that too. It didn't mean anything, other than when you looked at them, they never looked back.

But this was Sh'Nae and Ganns, and Darryl couldn't stop thinking that someone was getting hurt, because it sounded painful. He just didn't know to who. He wanted to rush in, to stop everything but that thought scared him. He looked around, and it was all strange. There was no smiling Sh'Nae, no windows to stare at Catalina Island out of, and no black microwave. Just strange places and strange noises.

In his heart, Darryl knew Ganns was at fault and that made him more frightened, because Ganns was in charge.

A male voice broke his thoughts. "Darryl? Is that you, Darryl?" They weren't making noises anymore. Still, there was something else. A streaming sound blossoming across the back of his head and overtopping his brain. It was like the static, but instead of turning it down someone was cranking the knob right. Darryl tried to shut the door again, but there was no knob, nowhere to grab. He reached to grab the door's edge, but in the dark he punched it open instead, and someone on the other side gasped. Darryl took a step back, his hands reflexively going to his ears, trying to block it all out. But the static swelled. This wasn't like the other times. This hurt.

He broke, first for the opposite wall, and on the way there he tripped across a small table and pulled it down. He looked up to see Ganns at the door, or partly at the door. His left half, one leg, some torso, one arm, and his head were all tension. His knees were bent, and he pushed his one arm, palm down, toward the floor, but his eyes were wide.

With one arm Darryl rolled the table away and sprung to his feet, searching. It was the door with the brass thing he needed. That was the exit, the way away from the noise. When he saw it, he also saw Ganns coming in, his nudity swinging, Darryl lowered a shoulder and bolted, hitting Ganns in the chest, then bouncing left. He then went for the exit.

Outside he found the afternoon hot, almost unbearably so, but he launched into it anyway. He'd spent enough time in hotels working for Ganns that he knew there'd be stairs, so he chose an end and ran. And ran. And ran some more. He hit the crash bar on the door at the bottom of the stairs to find the sun still bright. Straight across was a Flying J, and past that there was a field. They'd check the Flying J, even the stalls. Security used to find him in the stalls on cold nights and throw him out. Instead of running into the station, he rounded it and went into the field beyond.

The plants were green and leafy, but most importantly they were thick and knee-high. He went into the field maybe ten feet, and squatted, fighting the buzz the whole time. He tried to look, to see if either Ganns or Sh'Nae had come out the door, but he couldn't see that end of the hotel. With no clear direction he waited, picking up a leaf, focusing on it, and counting in a whisper.

Nine hundred and ninety-nine. Nine hundred and ninety-eight…

For a few seconds Sh'Nae shuffled her anxiety back as she walked through the Hotel Monteleone's lobby. Its old-world elegance was overwhelming, with the gold and glass chandeliers and multi paned windows looking down into the expansive, gingham pattern tiled foyer. Fluted pillars and colorful botanicals attempted to catch her attention, but the grandfather clock demanded it instead with its dark wood swirled by Gothic carvings. It took her breath away, but she took it back. She needed her breath, and she needed her wits, because Darryl was out there somewhere and Ganns was in conflict mode now. He wanted the police there before he found his pants, and Sh'Nae understood. If she thought it'd do any good, she would have made the call. But Darryl was an adult and there was little chance they'd do anything other than take his description. Instead, she convinced Ganns that they needed to change tack, that they needed to get to New Orleans before Darryl could. Ganns didn't get this either, he didn't understand why there weren't herding searches around the hotel, because there was no way that Darryl could have gotten far, because they were dressed and in the parking lot in less than ten minutes. But Sh'Nae knew. Darryl lived on the streets for years and if there was one thing he understood, innately, it was disappearing.

It got worse when she said they not only should not search, but they needed to get to New Orleans quickly.

"He's here. He's here! Why are we going there? He might not even continue without us."

"Stop," she said. "He will. He must. Darryl's one reliable trait is fixation, and when we left for New Orleans, the goal was cemented for him. He is as incapable of avoiding New Orleans as you are of understanding Judd Apatow."

Ganns crossed his arms, then finally shook his head and let them relax at his side. "I hate that shit."

"Darryl's running?"

"Judd Apatow. What's your plan after we get there? It's over a thousand miles and he's walking."

"He won't walk. and I keep telling you that he's not dumb. He's intuitive, one of the most intuitive men I've ever met. At least he is when he's focused."

"I don't know how you know that. He's not an idiot, but he's also not intelligent. I doubt he'd eat if you didn't put the food in front of him."

Thinking back to the day she'd met Darryl, his sitting next to a dumpster in the alley between 1st Street and 2nd, south of Mesa. She was scrawny and tired and confused, her head pounding with every step, and he was laughing at a fish head he'd pulled out of the dumpster. She watched him perform a one fish head puppet show for twenty minutes before he offered her one of the dumpster-sourced sandwiches piled at his knees.

She sat there, chewing as little as possible before swallowing, because she was sure the room temperature egg salad would kill her. But it hadn't.

"You don't know. You'll never know. Can we get moving now?" She didn't want to explain it anymore.

So now they were in New Orleans, at the hotel Ganns said he always stayed at when he visited the Crescent City. He got them two adjoining rooms, more out of habit than anything else, on the 14th floor, and on the elevator up he mentioned that the hotel was supposed to be haunted. That wouldn't matter to her, but it'd certainly matter to Darryl when they found him. They might have to move to another hotel, but she'd worry about that later. She was more worried about the "finding Darryl" part.

She suspected that he'd hitchhike, and that he'd hold out for a semi. Darryl had little faith in mankind, but he wasn't as suspicious as institutions, and trucking was an institution. Everything without a face was, and Darryl wouldn't see the face on trucking until he climbed up into the cab. Then it'd be too late.

That made her nervous as well, and nervousness forced her to plan.

"The earliest he'll be here is tonight, and I doubt that'll happen. He'll hide first." She said, then paused, thinking. "I expect he'll start hitchhiking before dawn tomorrow. Let's call that 5. If it takes, what, two hours? Then he'll be on the road by 7. That'd put him in New Orleans by about midnight tomorrow night, right?" She knew that wasn't exactly the answer, but exact answers were what Ganns lived for. She could give it to him.

He shook his head. "Chances are he's not going to find a fresh driver at 7 in the morning. Possible, but not probable. That means he'll have to find two rides, at least. I think truckers are more careful about picking up hitchhikers down along the border. Add some time for that. I think tomorrow evening is optimistic."

She nodded and kept nodding until he continued.

"I'm also guessing that he'll drive the drivers insane with his lists, which means he'll get dropped off at the first truck stop in the vicinity of New Orleans." He pulled out his phone and started searching. Sh'Nae smiled, just a little, and she hid it.

The first leg of his trip lasted longer than Ganns would have guessed, but otherwise he'd hit all the marks. Darryl didn't make for a good guest, as he was only willing to participate in the ride and nothing more. The driver who picked him, a plump Latina with big hair, began the trip with an inquisition. What's your name? Where are you from? Where are you going? Who are you running from? You are running, right? And so it went. Darryl tried to answer in short sentences, even single words, but he tried to answer. He had to give back something, but there wasn't much there in the swirl of his brain. Words flashed by, some which he was even able to pluck from the miasma.

"Long Beach" he said, when asked where he was from. That was the first city he thought of, the one across the green bridge from San Pedro. "Washington or California?" she asked. "I think there's one on the east coast, too. Dios mío! Such big beaches." Then she kept going with the questions, sometimes asking two or three before Darryl could answer the first. He tried, he tried hard, but by Allamoore he was rocking in his seat, she was silent, and the truck droned all the way to Houston. She sang sometime, beating on the steering wheel in time with music Darryl couldn't identify, and occasionally she looked over. The sides of her face tilted down at the edges, both eyes and mouth, and Darryl knew that face. He'd seen it many times on many people, and he still didn't know why. Did his own face do that? Was it doing it now and she was imitating him? He felt it, one hand running along the stubbly flesh, but if his mouth were turned down, he couldn't tell.

He knew they were there when she announced it, loudly and firmly, and then told Darryl that after she pulled into a truck stop that he had to pick up another ride. She didn't say that he was leaving, or why he was leaving, just that he needed another ride. Which meant the same thing, either way. If there was anything Darryl appreciated it was clarity, because clarity was rare.

There were different types of truck stops dotting the ribbon of asphalt from El Paso to Houston. The small ones, almost universally two-toned, were plentiful. Sometimes they were new, with their paint shiny, and a few even had some extra fat around the rear tires, but mostly they were old and square, with paint and patina and a slurry of stickers on the rear windows. He couldn't read stickers in truck stop parking lots from the highway, but there were plenty passing on the interstate to keep his searching eyes busy. Without exception, he found, they wore at least one with red, white, and blue colors and a single star. There were variations, of course. Some were the whole of the sticker in a rectangular shape. Others were in the shape of Texas. Sometimes it was just the colors and the sticker itself was a star. There were other stickers, and more of those disbelieved the media than anything else. It was a popular notion. Plenty mentioned the NRA, whatever that was. There were over a dozen stickers which mentioned an honor student, including one which said, very specifically, that "My Kid Sucked the Blood of Your Honor Student". Darryl wasn't sure why that was important, but he did appreciate the lowered, black Cadillac wearing it.

Here at the Gears 'N Gas Truck Stop the vehicles were largely boring and mostly little trucks. Mostly. There was a long, old car, one Darryl could almost pin a tag on. Almost. The handles on the driver's door and its associated passenger door were next to each other, and there was a name for that. He struggled, but then it came to him. "Suicide doors," that's what they were called. Suicide doors. There were plenty of spots in front of the stop, but the suicide doors were parked on the far side of the pumps, all alone and cattywampus across two slots. Darryl walked farther out, past the pumps, and stared at the suicide doors.

It wasn't lowered like the Cadillac was, but in every other way it was just as mean. The paint wore its patina with pride, reveling in the oxides and irregularities. Its wheels were brushed steel and filthy, the wide white walls stained. The windows were deeply tinted, like a black pearl buffed shiny. Darryl wanted to stare longer, but he didn't want to remain outside, in full view. While he doubted Ganns would be personally looking for him, he knew Sh'Nae would. She wouldn't let go. Ever.

He went inside.

The truck stop was broad and open, with something like a banister separating the dining room on the right from the rows of chocolate bars and CB antennas on the left. Darryl stood at the banister, one hand gripping the dark wood, and watched the people eating. He'd been moving too fast to think about eating until now, and he was hungry. It'd be okay, though. He'd been hungry before. He could eat in New Orleans.

He turned and walked directly into the chest of someone behind him, bouncing Darryl backward toward the banister. A large hand reached out, grabbed Darryl's shoulder, and steadied him.

"Watch yourself, son. You can hurt yourself like that." All Darryl saw, at first, were teeth. Two long rows of white, perfectly square teeth. There were lips framing them, but they were thin and nearly faded into the face. It was mostly just teeth.

"Hungry, son? Looks like you're hungry. I've got a table. Why don't you join me? They've got rib eyes and T-bones. Good beef here in Texas."

"Beef," said Darryl. "Beef," the man repeated. "Bottom sir loin, brisket, chuck, and flank," Darryl answered back. As he calmed his vision widened, and Darryl saw more of the man than just his teeth. He was tall, well over six foot, an elderly gentleman with a military haircut of gray and a familiar face. Darryl continued while the man nodded.

"Plank, ribs, round, shank, short loin, and sirloin." When Darryl finished, he gave the man a small smile.

"You're a regular butcher, you are. That's handy. Handy!" With pressure on his shoulder, the man turned Darryl right and toward the banister's opening and the restaurant inside. They walked together, the man's grasp guiding. Inside, the man took his hand back and turned, taking a couple longer steps to lead the way to a table with a single glass of milk and a small salad on it. The man sat by the salad and motioned for Darryl to take the opposite side. Darryl didn't sit, though.

"Lucinda?" the man said, his voice flowing. "One more of the same for my friend here?" The man waved at the booth end opposite of him. "Please, son. We're having the meatloaf, and Lucinda has sworn that it's the best thing on the menu. She gave me her promise."

"No milk, though? Please?"

"No milk, Lucinda. Get the man some sweet tea, if you will?"

Darryl looked at the seat. It wouldn't be the first time a stranger had fed him, but it'd been years since the last time. He remembered one thing, that meals came attached to commitments, like truck rides usually did. Sometimes it was just a conversation, other times it was worse. But the man looked familiar. He looked friendly. His smile was genuine. And Darryl was hungry, so he sat. The lady Lucinda brought him a glass of sweet tea and a salad directly after, and Darryl dug in. He ate, watching the man's chest as he chewed, but instead of talking the man also ate. They continued that way through the salads and, after Lucinda brought their meals, halfway into the meatloaf. Lucinda was right, it was delicious.

"I travel a lot, son. A lot. And I know the look of another traveler, one like me. Where you headed?"

Darryl spun the fork in his mashed potatoes, mixing the gravy in.

"Eastbound, right?"

He spun slower. The man fed him, and there was a cost.

There was always a cost.

"New Orleans," Darryl said. "I'm going to New Orleans."

"What for?"

"Ghosts. I'm supposed to see the ghosts." He took a bite of the potatoes, hoping that was enough, but it was never enough.

"Lots of ghosts in New Orleans, I suspect. Almost infinite ghosts. It feels like a haunted city. What are you going to do, count them?"

Filling his mouth with a fat fork of meatloaf, Darryl chewed and thought, then shook his head. He waited until he could swallow, swallowed it with sweet tea, and gave up a little more. "We're looking for a particular one, but I don't know who. Sh'Nae didn't tell me."

"Sh'Nae?"

"She is my friend."

"Where is she?" the man stopped, then shook his head. He took his own bite of the meatloaf and chewed slowly. Carefully. When he finished, he started back up. "We should go find your friend, then. You haven't said as much, so please excuse me if I'm wrong, but I'm thinking you're not certain how you're getting to New Orleans."

Darryl's eyes lit up. "You're going there?"

"I can go anywhere, son. Anywhere at all, and since New Orleans fits into anywhere, that's where I'm headed! Will you join me?"

Darryl was already nodding.

When they finished, after the man was done paying the bill and they were walking out the door, after the man pointed at the hot rod Lincoln and said that's mine, it finally occurred to Darryl to ask.

"What was your name, sir?"

"You can call me Sam. Sam Beckett. It's nice to meet you, Darryl."

Darryl furrowed his brow and bit his lower lip, but he kept walking toward the cool Lincoln with the suicide doors. The tall man unlocked the passenger door first and opened it, motioned Darryl in, then walked around to the driver's side. The engine started with a rumble and stayed there.

"To the Big Easy we go."

Nodding, Darryl sank into the soft leather seat and wondered how Mr. Sam Beckett knew his name.

They'd been driving for a few hours, with Sam singing along with the radio and Darryl mostly staring out the broad, rectangular passenger window. He'd never been to this part of the world, and it appeared to be all water to him. Not all water, but mostly. They'd been on a bridge, a single bridge, for the last fifteen minutes.

"Love that piano and the song's just perfect, isn't it? "Go to the Mardi Gras", well yes sir, we will! You ever hear of Professor Longhair, Darryl?"

In the time they'd been driving, Darryl had learned that Sam talked for the sake of talking. He asked questions which didn't need answering. He told other cars on the interstate what lane they belonged in. Since he'd left the street, Darryl hadn't heard words for no reason, because that wasn't the style of either Sh'Nae or Ganns. They spoke for meaning. Back on the street, yeah. There'd been plenty of useless words.

Sam kept going, but he changed subjects.

"Where I'm from, it's a much different world. Can you believe that Darryl? We're born, we grow, we live, and we die thinking that there's this world, this one world. It's big, right? And different. You don't have to go to Bangkok to find the strangeness, 'cause you can find it right here in Louisiana. Still, as much as New Orleans isn't Paris, it's still in the same world and strangeness is just a difference of degrees. I could prove it, if you wanted me to."

He paused.

"Darryl?"

Darryl turned to look at Sam, his broad shoulders filling up the black leather of the seat and his head just a little shy of the headliner. "Yes?"

"Do you want me to prove it?"

Darryl shook his head. He didn't need to know the differences, but Sam kept going, making Darryl wonder why he'd asked the question in the first place.

"The way to prove it, of course, is by showing you another world." He quit talking then, quizzically, and Darryl went back to staring out of the window.

They drove for a few more minutes before Sam took an exit at the end of the bridge and pulled into a broad concrete parkway spackled with semis. Toward one end was a building, another truck stop, and across the street there was a small church, one of a modern style with two low, square steeples. It didn't really look like a church at all, but that's what the sign said. After gassing up, Sam got back in behind the wheel, then turned to Darryl. "You want to get something to eat?"

Darryl shook his head, keeping his eyes out the window.

"We can shop some in there. Truck stops have some pretty cool things. Hula girl dolls that dance while you drive and breakfast jellies flavored like hot peppers."

Darryl shook his head again. He wanted Sam to stop talking, that's what he wanted. But that wasn't going to happen. Pursing his lips, Darryl pushed the thought away. "What year is this car?"

"This ol' Lincoln is a 1966. Landau roof on this puppy, just like the other ones."

"The other ones?"

"It's my fourth 1966 Lincoln. I'm fond of them. Listen to that big block growl. There are no more rides like this in my time." He paused, but only long enough for Darryl to think, not long enough for Darryl to interrupt. "But you don't care about cars, I know that. I know you better than you think, in a manner."

The turn of words gave warning to Darryl, and he clenched his hands, waiting for the buzz to begin. It didn't, though. The sunshine came in his window, warming his face, and the trees continued on. It wasn't enough, and his shoulders sagged.

"It'll be different this time, because I've learned things."

Still no buzz. "Why do you keep buying the same kind of car, over and over?" he finally asked. It was better than just sitting there and listening. Would New Orleans never arrive?

"I don't. I've bought the exact same car four times over. Each car bought in the same place at the same time. Same salesman, too. I've really come to love it." He poked the accelerator, revving the engine, and Darryl slumped lower in his seat.

"You'll get it, Darryl. It's your first time, but there were other Darryls before. No hurry. If it makes you feel better, only some of this is familiar to me. If it were all familiar, then I'd be failing again. I'm okay with failing sometimes, because I have infinite opportunities."

Darryl waited for Sam to go on, because he would. As he waited, he unexpectedly slept. This was obvious when he woke up, his chin pressed against the window and the corner of his mouth soggy. It was dark outside, but there were lights. Lots of lights. He startled, banging his head against the window in the process. For a second he didn't know where he was, at least until Sam laughed. "Welcome back, Darryl. We're here!"

There were buildings, some shiny and silver, some yellowish, still others blue in the glum of night. The freeway was humming with traffic, mostly trucks, but also with the world of rounded cars that all looked the same to Darryl. It was New Orleans; he could feel it. He suspected that somewhere here Ganns and Sh'Nae either were or would be looking for him, but they could just keep on looking. It looked like a big city, with lots of nooks and crannies. They may need each other, but they didn't need him, and he didn't need them. Though now, he couldn't remember why.

"This is where we shift, my friend. This is where we try it again. Tonight, we're not getting a hotel, not the Courtyard and not that gorgeous Hotel St. Marie. Tonight, we change trails by sleeping sans. That's the word, I think. We're sleeping at Walmart! I'd love to have a better plan, but maybe it's the tangential shift we don't want, but need. These seats are pretty comfy, too."

"We're sleeping in the car?"

"Right. We're sleeping in the car. Don't let that worry you none, because sleep is temporary and we're going permanent. We have big plans for tomorrow, when the sun comes up. Big plans."

CHAPTER THREE

Year: 2317
Location: Near Chicago, Illinois

The woman sounded smart but looked sloppy, so Sh'Nae suspected that she didn't give a shit about first impressions. Her thick, red hair was only partly piled atop her head and her full red lips stained her doughy face. Sh'Nae couldn't help but wrinkle her nose at the thought.

I'm shallow, she thought, but then sometimes she was.

"Stop," Ganns said, interrupting her with a talk-to-the-hand motion. "STOP. When you called me, you said you could help, and that's what I want to hear about. Anything else and we're stiffing you with the coffees and walking."

"Darryl," she said. Her face didn't change, there was no expression, no emotion, no effusion, just the word "Darryl." But that was enough to clear Sh'Nae's preconceived notions with one sweep.

"Darryl?"

The woman nodded, putting a little bounce in her bangs, almost enough to reduce her ascetic demeanor. "To save us time, I'm going to explain the next 24 hours in about thirty seconds, and you won't believe it. Let me give you two my phone number now. That way you'll have it if you decide to walk away." At this she reached down into her purse, pulled out a slip of paper, and slid it to Sh'Nae, "What'll probably happen here is that I'll explain, you'll get up and leave, and you won't see me again until tomorrow morning. Between now and tomorrow morning, something will change your mind, and you'll call me." At this she pointed at Sh'Nae, then she turned her pointing finger at Ganns. "You're still going to be surly, but since you're still concerned about Darryl you won't leave again. From there we'll work to fix his problem."

"His problem? Where is Darryl? That's all I want to know." Ganns was using his stern voice, the one he used to shut down audience members who broke the rules.

"It doesn't have to play the way I just described, but if you change it up, I can't tell you if you'll ever learn anything more about Darryl. I'll not know any more than you at that point."

Sh'Nae leaned forward, pinching the slip of paper between one finger and her thumb until they hurt. "Are you threatening him?"

"I'm not, I'm on your side, sort of. The man he's with is not. Do you intend to walk or not? Tell me. I have other options."

Ganns leaned back and took a deep breath. "Options for what?" he asked softly.

"I'm not here to help you and I'm not here to help Darryl. I'm here to stop the man who is going by the name Sam Beckett. He's with Darryl right now."

"He has Darryl? Is he dangerous?"

"He doesn't have Darryl, because Darryl's with him voluntarily and he's not going anywhere. Is Sam dangerous? Depends on your perspective. For you, no. For Darryl, yes. For the future of all worlds, absolutely."

"Sam Beckett. Samuel Beckett. As in the "Waiting for Godot" Samuel Beckett?" Ganns dropped his offense at this point, which meant something the woman said was working. That or he had a hunch. Ganns often worked from hunches.

"I thought of someone else. He was on television. I think it was time travel, but I'm not sure. I was too young to really get it."

"Good memory, because *Quantum Leap* is where Sam got his nom de guerre. This is where I start my story, okay? Before I start though," she pointed at Ganns. "You want pie. They don't have razzleberry

36

because they don't know what razzleberry is, but they do have cherry." Waving her hand up in the air to get the waiter's attention, she finished. "Order it. You like it."

"This isn't freaky at all." Sh'Nae said. She had her eyes locked on the lady, trying to read what was inside, but it wasn't working. If the lady owned one emotion, one nerve, it hadn't shown yet. "What's your name, miss?"

"I'm Alex."

Sh'Nae leaned back, shoulder to shoulder with Ganns. He ordered the cherry pie, his face passive. On anyone else she'd guess it was apathy, but with him it meant focus. He was thinking and thinking hard. She guessed it was her job to keep Alex talking until Ganns figured out what to do.

"Yeah. Sure. Start already."

"Thank you. To begin, we've met before. We've been through these questions before and that's how I knew about the pie, Patriot Ganns.

"Here's the hardest part. To explain why I'm here, I have to tell you where I'm from. That's where our relationship sours, but I don't know how else to do it. I'm not a salesman and I'll never get you into a new car or an old god." She stopped for a second, stirring her coffee. She played with the mug, turning back and forth, but never lifted it off the table.

"I started out as a scientist, goddamn it. I think like a scientist. This is agent shit."

While she was listening to the lady, Sh'Nae was really paying attention to Ganns. This trip would go the way he went, and that was the way of things when you were with Ganns. She didn't really think of their relationship as being based on trading sugar, because ninety percent of what they did together was business and only ten percent was naked. But there was sugar involved, regardless of how she thought of it, and that made times like this, where he had the force of personality, weird. They'd go where he wanted and do what he wanted, because he was the boss with the vision and the money.

She watched the boss, and he was warming up to the lady. Instead of leaning back in the booth, he was sitting up, and he had both arms on the table. Most importantly, he nodded and watched the lady. He was invested, for some reason.

"What kind of scientist?" he asked.

"Mutagnomologist." She quit spinning the cup and grasped it with both hands, as if warming herself.

"Never heard of it."

"No, you wouldn't have. It won't be invented for several more generations."

And Ganns leaned back.

"See? That's what I mean. Now I've only inferred three times that I'm not from your world, but you've already given up on me."

"That means you're, what? An alien?"

"No, I'm human, like you. From earth, like you. Just a different earth."

"A different earth. Why would you expect us to believe in a different earth?"

"Have we ever met, before now?"

"Yeah, you know what kind of pies I like. You've heard of Darryl, and you know we're looking for him. Not enough. A twenty-four-hour news cycle and the Internet has made the world irretrievably small."

"When you were a child, you were caught torturing a turtle by someone, a family member, I think. I didn't get his name, but he was a big man, with a thick belly hanging out and shorts cut raggedly. Long, stringy hair."

Ganns leaned forward. "Black hair? That was my uncle, my father's brother. He lived in Oklahoma."

"You were holding up a small turtle by one leg and poking your fingers at its face every time it stuck it out, but it always retreated. At first you were laughing, but then you grew frustrated, then angry. You threw the turtle down several times, and it always tried to crawl away, and you grabbed a leg again.

"Your uncle, he came up behind you and grabbed the turtle out of your hands, tossing it like a discus into the lake, and you were angry at him. You yelled and yelled that you wouldn't leave until the turtle came back."

Ganns didn't say anything, but Sh'Nae turned to look at him anyway. Finally, he asked "can you tell me what my uncle's name was?"

"No, I never asked him. Or you. Until a few seconds ago, I didn't know he was your uncle. I only described what I saw."

"What you saw? That was probably fifty-five years ago. You're not old enough."

"Thank you." She took a sip of coffee, set it down, then picked up her napkin and started carefully tearing it down one long edge. When she finished, she took a piece of what she tore and laid it out.

"People think of time like this, as a line." She dipped a finger in her coffee, then touched the strip close to its left edge. "This is where you lost your turtle friend." She dipped her finger again and touched it in the middle. "This is the three of us, right now." She dipped one last time and touched the strip on the far right. "This is where I'm from." Then she picked up the strip, wadded it, and dropped it on the table. "Except it's not like that. Not at all."

"You're from the future? What's your full name, Alex?"

Ganns asked. Sh'Nae kept staring at the wadded-up strip and the napkin which had been its parent. Not answering, Alex picked up the little box of sugar packets, a small porcelain container in the shape of a rectangle. Stuffed inside were pink and white and blue single serving packets of sweeteners, but they didn't stay there. The woman turned the rectangle upside-down and dumped them on the table beside the ketchup. Then she held the container up before Ganns and Sh'Nae.

"This is time, in a fashion. Imagine this container infinitely wide and infinitely long. The shape doesn't really matter, what matters is that you stop thinking linearly. Think in terms of volume."

"What's your name?" Ganns persisted.

"Imagine that inside this shape is the entire world. I come along forty years ago and, instead of watching your uncle toss your turtle, I shoot him to prevent him from interceding. Your life changes because of that turtle and maybe because of the loss of your uncle, and now there's a new timeline."

"How very Stephen King of you," Sh'Nae said. She was tired of being left out.

"The butterfly effect," Ganns said, matter-of-factly.

"Not really, Ganns. The butterfly effect isn't an effective explanation. Its focus is that small things can have big impacts, and in the multiverse, that's not correct. The size of the initiator is irrelevant because it's only the result which matters. For example, I can swap these," she picked her spoon out of her coffee and laid it on the table. Then she picked up her fork and put it in the coffee where the spoon had been. "And if our meeting goes on as it has been, it won't matter one iota. On the other hand, if we suddenly need a weapon and grab one, the wrong one, and things go awry, maybe my swapping them did matter. The same goes with me shooting your uncle. It might have mattered, or it might not have."

"Don't shoot my uncle who's been dead for thirty years."

"You're missing my point, and my name is Alex. Alex Donna.

"Let's assume I kill your uncle and it does have a result. You love animals and the environment and instead of making movies you go into politics to save the world. What happens in here?" She shakes the sugar receptacle.

"No idea," Sh'Nae said. She was hooked.

She pointed the container at Ganns. "Inside here there's the world we know now, and inside the container there's now a new world, one which develops different from the point where your uncle died. They both fit in here, at the same time. Afterward, if I go back and don't kill your uncle but do kill your turtle, there's now a third world. Again, all fitting in here nicely."

"I think there's a rule of physics against all this. Conservation of something." Ganns sounded perturbed, but he looked completely wrapped up in Donna's presentation. Sh'Nae nodded. She didn't know about the physics, but it didn't sound right.

"Conservation of mass, and no. Theoretically, and considered on a scale set by universes, it's the same mass. The hardest part to swallow is that you're the same guy in all three worlds, but now you're doing different things in each. It's not really different worlds, it's the same world with different realities."

"What if I died in one of them?"

"All the worlds go on."

"How many go on?"

"It's possible that there could be infinite realities and infinite Ganns, but not really. At some point variations of possibility are so similar that they couldn't end up in a different result. Even then, the number is enormous. Almost unfathomable."

"Stop," Sh'Nae said. "One Ganns is enough. I want to hear about Darryl, and not infinite Darryls. I want the one in this reality."

"Of course. Ultimately, we're on the same side. I want to stop Beckett and you want to find Darryl. Those two go hand in hand."

"Why is that?" Ganns asked. "What's Beckett doing?"

She set the sugar container down and thought for a second.

"There are groups who believe that their reality is the best reality, that the people in all the other realities are suffering or evil or idiots or something else. These groups have been working for a long time, for decades, to collapse all realities into one. They largely try to collapse them all into their own, because they believe theirs is the correct one."

"Sounds like people," Ganns said. "Assuming I could buy in to multiple realities, this rings true. Tell us about Beckett. What does he want the world to be?"

"From my perspective, he wants anarchy. From his, I have no idea. Look, I'm here to execute my mission, and that's it. I want to stop Beckett. In doing so we'll recover Darryl, which means my mission should be your mission. I should add that if I don't stop Beckett, then Darryl will die. His death is necessary for Beckett to get his way."

"That sounds like a threat," Sh'Nae said, leaning forward.

"Call it what you want. To me, it's simply the truth."

"Why not just move on to a reality that's not a problem for you, then? Why go through this trouble?" Ganns couldn't let his doubt go.

"Because it's a mission. An assignment." She shook her head. "You're not understanding."

"I understand," Sh'Nae said. "And Ganns does as well. More than you know. And whether I believe your bullshit or not, I'll help you just to stay close to you. But understand something, if you're using us, I'll find a way to get even. You'll probably just change realities and come back anyway, but I'll feel better."

"That's not likely," Donna said.

"Why is that?"

"If I die, that version of me can't be there to change the reality, which means that version of me remains dead." She crossed her arms, but her face remained passive. "This job takes commitment."

"So does the night shift at 7-Eleven," Sh'Nae said. "For the same reason."

"It'll feel like a dream," Alex said. "At least at first. It's just like an alarm clock, once you're used to it."

Sh'Nae sprawled on the floor, listening to Alex talk. It was like her voice wasn't real, like it was being whispered into one of Sh'Nae's ears. She looked around, at the walls and the floor, and it all looked like nothing. The color was a uniform eggshell and the room's features were uniformly featureless.

They hadn't walked out on Alex and her story like she said they would, they'd remained, and they'd listened and they'd argued. Maybe it was Alex's patience or maybe it was her honesty about her focus being on Beckett. Maybe it was just that she and Ganns didn't have a better answer on finding where Darryl went and, from what Alex said, they would continue to not find Darryl. In any case, she'd been willing to come back to Ganns' hotel room instead of going to her own. That gave Ganns the degree of security he felt he needed. She also made it a point to show that she wasn't armed, which also helped.

Back at the hotel, she'd explained a bit more about what they were about to do. She called it shifting and said that everyone in the world was capable of doing it. The reason the rest of the world didn't do it was that it was largely a secret kept tight by those who could, and because the number of folks who could do it without science (she called them "naturals") was very small. "In a world of billions, there are only twenty or thirty thousand who can shift naturally at any one time, and I'm not one of those," she said. "Neither are either of you." At this point she handed each a small, round tin. They were about as big around as a golf ball and half an inch thick, like a baby hockey puck. When you rotated the top of the puck enough, it had a hole in the side which lined up with a hole in the bottom of the puck, and a small white pill fell out. Ganns held it up, squinting, and asked "is that a cross top?" Alex ignored him. She said they'd need to take one every time they shifted, because it opened their mind. If they could figure out how to open their mind without it, then they'd be naturals. She also said that never happened. You were either a natural and knew it, or you weren't. Period.

"My head hurts," a male voice said. She couldn't see Ganns, but he had to be close.

"Where are we?" she asked.

"Chicago," Alex said, leaning over her. "Take my hand." Sh'Nae did, gathering herself to sit.

"When are we?" Ganns asked. He was behind her, she guessed.

"2317. My 2317. Come on, let's get you guys checked in."

They made small talk as they went between multiple stations. At first there was a chance to shower and change, but they'd all met in an empty corner of the Carousel Bar and Lounge, not an hour after Sh'Nae and Ganns awoke, finished making love, and prepared for the day. They could skip showers.

It was obviously a government affair, because after the showers came an eight-foot metal table with two chairs and a stack of forms in front of each of them. They were pecking away at the stacks when Ganns broke the silence.

"Huh," he said. "That's a first."

"What's that?" Sh'Nae only had two left and didn't want to be slowed down.

"Race. They never asked about race."

She looked at him, trying to figure out where he was going with this.

"Have you ever filled out a government form and not answered a question about race?"

"I don't know that I ever paid attention. Don't read so much into it, Ganns. It's government paperwork."

Ganns set his pencil down and shot Sh'Nae an exasperated face. "Really? Really? Look around you, Sh'Nae. This isn't a government building or research lab. This is a set, and a poor one at that. This is the future? Where's the machine that goes 'ping'? It's all bullshit!"

"Bullshit?" She looked around.

"Bullshit. The headache? We were drugged. Alex's knowledge? Suggestion or hypnosis. I don't know what, but I know it's bullshit."

She couldn't let it go, but to deescalate, she metered her voice. "You came along. Voluntarily."

Breathing deep, Ganns nodded. "I did, but only because this has to, in some way, lead to Darryl."

"Yesterday you thought he was still on the road."

"I don't believe in coincidences, okay? She showed up out of nowhere."

"Yeah, she did." Sh'Nae set her pen down and leaned back in her chair. "So now what? Either her story is true and may lead to Darryl, she's full of shit and may lead to Darryl, or, I don't know. This is candid camera and her last name is Funt? What then?"

Ganns rolled his eyes. "You're not old enough to know about Allen Funt, right?" He frowned. "You don't think we have a choice? Is that what you're telling me?"

"I don't see one."

"Fine." Ganns picked up his pen. "Fine. We keep going." He looked up at the ceiling "You hear that?! We keep going!"

After they finished their paperwork, they were left waiting for a quarter hour before Alex returned carrying a small box, which she identified as a recorder. She asked if she could record their conversation, and Sh'Nae nodded assent for them both.

"Up until now, all we've planned on was going to find and retrieve Darryl. What's more important is the timing. If we take him away too early, it won't matter, and we'll repeat this exercise. If we take him away too late, he'll be dead. We have to time this, and because of that there's going to be a delay."

"We're early, then?" Sh'Nae asked.

"Yes, we're early. In a way. In shifting, you can go from anywhere to anywhere, but to succeed you must choose your points right. We think we know where we need to be, but we're going to check it before we go. Just being safe."

"The future's changed, and that means we're in a new world. That's what you described," Ganns said.

"It is," Alex said, nodding. "Let's keep going. You've read CARNIVAL OF FURY, right?"

"I did. How did you know?"

"Because I mailed it to you. The goal was to get you interested in New Orleans and the Robert Charles riots."

Ganns turned to Sh'Nae and raised one eyebrow, his see what I mean look, and Sh'Nae nodded. She was trying to decide if she should be angry. "We didn't lose Darryl until we were on the way to New Orleans. If you hadn't mailed it, he'd still be with us."

"Not true. In the previous reality he was taken off the street, before I mailed the book to Ganns. He disappeared, with you and Ganns never seeing him again."

"Oh bullshit," Ganns said. "You say that because you can say that. We can't prove you wrong, but we don't have to believe." He crossed his arms. "We don't have to."

"You're right, but if you don't it doesn't change anything. We still need to figure out the best way to interrupt plans the presentists have with Darryl. They won't let him just walk away, and there's more of them than us. We'll have better weapons, though."

"Jesus," Sh'Nae said. "Why would they want Darryl?"

"Wait, Sh'Nae. I'm not ready to leave her setting us up yet."

"Remember when you first saw Darryl, Sh'Nae?"

Sh'Nae didn't mind Ganns. "Sure."

"Let me tell you about it, okay? You can jump in anytime, Ganns, but you won't be able to because you don't know it all. Sh'Nae does, because she was there. I do, because I watched. And you won't know, because I doubt Sh'Nae has ever told you."

"Go ahead and tell me, then," Sh'Nae said, her voice dropping.

"Downtown San Pedro is riddled with alleyways, ones which are comparatively clean and orderly compared to some cities, but at night they can still become dangerous, shadowy places. You first saw Darryl in one of these alleys, down by 3rd and Mesa. You started in the alley, but you two ended up in a dumpster."

Sh'Nae didn't respond.

"The dumpsters for downtown business sit in the alleys, and where they can they're tucked into cubbies built into the building walls. You were probably looking for a place to sleep, right? You found Darryl and you found he was eccentric. He was also entertaining. After you two talked, you decided to sleep in the dumpster."

"You slept in a dumpster? With Darryl?" Ganns asked Sh'Nae.

"It was drizzling, and the dumpster was dry. I'm a light sleeper, so I knew it was safe. Plus, it wasn't a restaurant dumpster and it didn't stink much. It was mostly boxes. I also wanted to know why he'd started crying."

"But you slept in a dumpster?"

"You knew we lived on the street when you met us."

"I'm not judging. I just," he looked up, searching for how he felt. "I just didn't know."

Sh'Nae nodded, not really listening to Ganns now. "Funny how I couldn't take care of myself, but I thought I could take care of someone else."

"Why was Darryl crying?" Alex asked.

"All he told me was that he didn't know where he was. That he was lost. I thought maybe he'd hurt himself."

Ganns had dropped his defensive posture and now was nodding along as Sh'Nae spoke.

"I asked him what he could remember, and he told me about places he'd slept, and I recognized most of them. Thinking maybe I could find him some family, I asked him if he was from there, and he said that he wasn't. But he didn't know where he was from. He only knew where he came from was warmer."

"Did you learn about his seeing ghosts then?" Ganns asked.

"Kind of? I think that was part of it."

"Why is that?"

"We slept sitting up in one corner, with him snuggled under my arm. At least, that's how I slept. I don't know if he ever did, because he was awake when I fell asleep and awake when I awoke. He spent the night staring opposite us, at the other end of the dumpster. And he kept drawing his legs up tight, then relaxing, then drawing them up again. I didn't think about it then, but now I believe he was seeing something. We were on the street, right? I let it go as the crazy."

"The crazy?" Alex asked.

Sh'Nae nodded at her. "Ganns hates it when I say that, but it's rampant on the streets, and all of it is different. After a while you don't spend time classifying the peculiarities, you just call it the crazy and move on."

"This is really what we needed to get to, things about Darryl and things that'll help us come up with a strategy."

"If he sees me, he'll come to me. I know that."

"They have a relationship," Ganns said. He looked pensive.

"In that world, probably. There you mothered him for years. But he's elsewhere now, and that can change how things work in one's head," Alex said.

"Elsewhere?" Ganns asked, but the door opened up as he did, and a man walked in.

He was a young fellow with clear eyes, a tall neck, and taller hair. He moved smoothly, like a swan, flowing into one of the chairs at the single large table in their room.

"Time for a break. Sh'Nae and Ganns, this is Doctor Looman. He'll be giving you a medical briefing." She sat down next to him as the man reached for the two piles of paper. "Sh'Nae Mosley," he said, locking eyes with her. Sh'Nae nodded.

"Patriot Ganns," he said, looking at Ganns.

"Just Ganns."

"Certainly, Mr. Ganns."

"No, just Ganns. Nothing before and nothing after. Just Ganns."

The doctor nodded, his tall neck and pinched eyes accentuating his thinness. His lab coat could've been held up by a wire hanger. "Just Ganns. Got it. We're going to talk about complications associated with shifting, of which there are primarily three."

"Primarily?" Sh'Nae asked.

"There can be exceptions. Sometimes there are symptoms, like nausea or vertigo, but when it comes to lasting effects there are only three: dysthymia, anosognosia, and a form of dysplasia called neoheplastic asphyxiation. We can tell already that you aren't suffering from anosognosia and the dysthymia is easily treated, should you show signs. To ensure you're not suffering from NAS, we'll need some blood samples."

"What if I don't want to give blood samples?" Ganns said. "Because I don't."

"It's your choice, of course," said Alex. "We won't force you. But NAS is terminal."

"I don't frighten, Alex."

"I don't care, Ganns. I'm not trying to frighten you. I'm a scientist and a cold fish, much the opposite of you. I'd recommend you take the blood panel. We can't help neoheplastism if we don't know about it. If you don't, I don't care."

Reaching over, Sh'Nae put a hand on Ganns' shoulder. "I don't need to worry about you, too."

"I don't know what to believe and I don't know what to do. How do you?"

"I don't. Not anymore than you do. I just don't see any downside to giving them blood, even if they're lying. Do you?"

"I don't know."

"Yes, yes you do. You know if there's a specific fear or a suspicion. What is it?"

"It's everything."

"Then you're willing to die, maybe? Because of everything? Quit dodging me, Ganns."

Doctor Looman leaned forward, putting his hands on the table and looking back and forth between the two. "I'll be honest, Ganns. With you being in here, we already know everything we want to know about you. Your blood won't help or hurt us, so just make up your mind." Unused to bluntness from anyone besides Sh'Nae, Ganns stared at the doctor with his mouth half open.

"He'll take the blood test, Dr. Looman. He'll take the goddamned blood test."

"Sh'Nae can't give me permission for you." The doctor said to Ganns, shaking his head.

Ganns nodded. "Fine. Like she said, I'll take the goddamned blood test. That thing, nehohep…"

"Neoheplastic ashphyxiation syndrome, but we call it NAS."

"What is it?" Ganns finished.

"Healthy livers regenerate, With NAS, your liver does more than regenerate, it grows. Quickly. And it never stops growing. Eventually it crowds your lungs and you asphyxiate."

"Jesus," Sh'Nae whispered.

"We can slow it, but it's not treatable. Diagnosis results in full-time hospitalization. It's miserable and most patients request euthanasia."

"I don't want to hear anymore," said Ganns.

"How often does this happen?" Sh'Nae didn't look frightened, she looked interested.

"Maybe once every fifty thousand made shifts." Dr. Looman looked at Alex. "Did you explain made shifts?"

"Not in detail. He," she flicked a finger toward Ganns, "wasn't in a listening mood. But they've heard about naturals."

"Naturals do this thing" Sh'Nae waved one hand about in the air, "naturally. I guess that means made shifts require science. Like that pill we took?" Alex nodded. "It's a hypnotic drug to enhance the power of suggestion, that's the science. Everyone can travel, but most need the drug to do so."

"Suggestion is powerful." Ganns said.

"Research shows that less than one percent of people are naturals, probably a lot less than one percent. It also indicates that about fifty percent of people, even given the drug, can't figure it out," Alex said. "With more rigorous mental exercises, we're able to get anyone we want traveling, though. That's why we believe everyone to be capable of it." He stood up. "I'm going to order your labs, then you shouldn't have to see me again." The doctor walked away.

"You guys could work on your bedside manner," Ganns said to Alex.

"Why would we?" Alex asked.

"You came back to get us, remember?"

"It's my job."

"Traditional government worker, then?"

"Maybe." She stood up this time. "There are five rooms in here, all empty. Take what you want. Meals are at eight, one, and seven, but if you ring that bell," she pointed at a red-painted buzzer next to the door, "someone will come help you. You can eat anytime you want. I'll be back after the test results are in."

"Can't we hurry?" Sh'Nae asked. "What if Darryl's in trouble?"

"You just moved through three hundred years. Three days won't be a problem." Alex gave a small wave bounded by a sarcastic smile, then she left through the same door the doctor had exited through.

Ganns sat at the table, his shoulders hunched and head hanging. Sh'Nae waited for the inevitable, but when it didn't come, she sat beside him. That worked.

"I can't see it," Ganns mumbled, his head still down.

"See what?"

He looked up and waved around. "What all this is for. The reason. That's the thing in science fiction that always failed me— the reason." Sh'Nae wanted to say that things just are sometimes, but instead she nodded and put a hand on one of his knees.

"I don't know how to play them if I don't understand why they're doing whatever the hell it is they're doing. I don't know." He stood and began pacing the room. "I can't say that out loud, but I don't know why. I'm sure they're listening to us now." He looked up. "They know me already." His next pass by the table he sat quickly, leaning in to

Sh'Nae and whispering, "but I know some things." She leaned into him as well.

"I know that they'll come back and tell one of us, I don't know which, but one of us, that we've got the liver thing. Then whatever it is they do for it, they'll do that. It'll be to separate us." She knew it was useless, but that didn't stop Sh'Nae. It couldn't stop her. "Does that make sense to you? Why? Why would they do that?"

He raised his head, boring holes through her resolve with his glare. "I. Don't. Know." While his glare was anger, she heard something else in his voice. She heard pleading. He needed her to believe, and she wanted to. But unlike him, she needed a reason. She also needed to know that they would go forward, that they would be finding Darryl.

"If you don't know why, explain why you're stuck on this."

"You never just believe, do you? No. You never will just believe, and you will never just go with how you feel. That's not you. It needs to be all be processed and parsed." He shook his head, and she knew he was done talking. Logic failed Ganns, as it always had.

The afternoon went slow and tepid. First, they gave blood, then they ate lunch, a plate of cold cuts Sh'Nae didn't recognize with a loaf of bread and three different condiments, all of which tasted like variations of mustard. Which was fine because she hated mayonnaise. Though it hardly seemed like the drink of the future, they also got a pitcher of fruit punch. Ganns picked at the meats, trying each of the choices before choosing the marbled one, but he scowled with every bite.

He was angry. Angry with Sh'Nae for buying into the bullshit alternative universe story and angry with himself for not knowing how to unlatch her from it. He knew she saw it as unlatching from Darryl's safety, which wasn't going to happen. He knew that they were using her commitment as bait for him, and that was infuriating. Most of all, Ganns knew he was powerless, and that made him angry. He had no cards to play. Until now he'd told himself they were both business partners, with his dalliance with Sh'Nae being a side benefit, but since Darryl's disappearance he realized there was more to it than that. It was more than his anger over Alex's manipulation of Sh'Nae, it was his own fear that Darryl was somehow eclipsing him in Sh'Nae's world.

It would continue, though. Alex would do what she did and Sh'Nae would follow her heart to wherever she thought Darryl to be. On reflection, he realized that made him the fifth wheel.

"It'll be me," he said, to no one in particular.

"What?" Sh'Nae asked.

"It'll be me," Ganns said, offering a wan smile. "They'll pick me."

After Sh'Nae went to take a nap, Ganns sat at the table, picking at the lunch meats and growing maudlin. Since they'd met Alex, the ride felt like a runaway locomotive to him. They were on a track, but not one he had any control over. And he knew they were moving way too fast.

Part of Ganns also knew that his reluctance was born in his lack of control. He'd been following his heart, which meant following Sh'Nae while chasing Darryl, even though he knew she was blindly following Alex to find her friend. That's where it all burned. His brain told him that it was all manipulation by Alex and her friends, but his heart told him he had to stick with Sh'Nae, because he had to save her from them. He knew her heart was following Darryl, and Darryl was important. To both of them, really.

Important?

It wasn't about his importance. It couldn't be. Ganns acknowledged that, without Darryl, Second Sight Pictures wouldn't have even been a vision. Yeah, he was important. But, first, Darryl was a human. He deserved better than being a commodity, whether it be for Alex or for Second Sight. Plus, Alex's words told Ganns that Darryl was in danger. This was more than the loss of an asset. This might be the loss of a life. If he didn't see it through, it'd certainly be the loss of a potential relationship he thought, for the moment, worth living for.

The door cracked and an older man stuck his head in. "Can I clean up a bit, sir? I came for the plates." His came through, not waiting for an answer, but Ganns nodded his assent anyway. The man's head was skeletal, except for the wattle beneath his chin. He's ancient, Ganns thought. He was a short fellow, his back a little stooped and his legs bowed as if his knees rejected each other.

But he moved quick and his eyes glinted. Instantly Ganns liked the fellow.

"Any good news today, fellow?" Ganns broached.

The man shrugged. "There's muskie back in Lake Michigan. I heard it on the vid. It's been a long time." he waved one hand back behind him. "Good for the pikes." He dragged a canvas bag behind him, and Ganns saw the cloth was stained and its insides clinked. He came to the table and began dropping the dirty plates into the bag without reservation. "How about you?" he added at the end. "Any good in here?"

"My lady," Ganns nodded back at one of the side rooms, "she's napping. She has that coming."

"We all do. How come you're out here, then?" He stopped at the platter with the cold cuts, holding it an inch off the table. Ganns waved it off, and the platter went into the bag as well.

"Just thinking."

"It's hard to think in here. Too sterile. You need yourself some sunlight." The man's words made Ganns smile.

"You got that right," he said.

Pulling a tan cloth out of his waistband, the man wiped the table. "So why don'tcha go get some?"

"Excuse me?" Ganns asked.

"Getcha some. There's the door." He pointed back the way he came.

"But I'm waiting for something." Regardless, Ganns eyed the door anyway.

"Of course, you are. All y'all do. When you're ready, there it is."

"It's just open?" Ganns asked.

"Sure? What'ja think?" the man turned away and started back the way he'd come. "This ain't a jail."

"I can come and go as I please?"

The man pointed back the way he came. "I guess." He walked over, opened the door, and shut it again. "No key for me. Out and left, then straight to the front of the building. You taking the guest with you?"

"Guest?"

"You're from there, then. Okay. The lady you came with, is she going?"

"She's sleeping right now. Why?"

"She can't have any privacy, is all. You two can wander around, but with her you'll both be watched."

That was when it dawned on Ganns that he'd not seen one black person yet. Or a brown one.

Everyone was white.

He took a shot at it. "You call black people guests? Why is that?"

"Because when they're in the north that's what they are. Nothing wrong with it, or wrong with them, fella. Just that they're guests here. When we go there, we're the guests. You going to eat them?" he pointed at a bowl of crackers.

"Yes, leave them." Ganns wasn't listening anymore. He was thinking about here and there. It only took a few moments for him to decide he needed to know what here was. "I think I will take a walk."

"Suit yourself." The man dragged his sack out the door and walked away.

Ganns stood to follow, then looked back at the door behind which Sh'Nae was probably sleeping. Probably. She could have been listening for all Ganns knew, but she was probably sleeping. She could sleep almost anywhere.

She'd be safe. He didn't trust these people, and he didn't trust a word they said, but he hadn't felt threatened. At least, he hadn't felt she'd been threatened. Alex was much more interested in Sh'Nae than she was in him. Ganns was largely the fifth wheel, an irritated and suspicious fifth wheel.

Out the door and to the left he went.

Buildings hadn't changed all that much between the centuries and realities. The floor was flecked cream tile with black cove molding, and the walls were sterile white. A few pictures hung on them, some with places and some with people, but Ganns didn't care about either. He kept his eyes on the door ahead. The hallway ahead was empty. There was a desk and counter at the front, both made of chromed metal and a dark blue, matte material. No one sat behind the desk, there were no papers and no monitors. Nothing. It was like the furniture was just moved in.

He'd told Sh'Nae that it was a set, and a poorly built one, and it continued to look like one to him. They could have at least strewed a few papers about. Maybe a pencil. Something just to make it look like someone had been working. A monitor with a blinking cursor would go a long way, too. But no. Nothing.

He kept going, past the desk and out the door. The sun outside was warm and suddenly he felt the rush of home. It was the world he knew, he felt that. The earth, the sun, the air, it was all familiar. It didn't smell like New Orleans, but the air was thick with humidity and smelled of foliage. It was probably still Louisiana, and New Orleans was probably not far away. There were sounds, insects he didn't recognize and the flick of birds in the trees, but he didn't hear anything mechanized. No traffic. How far from the city did you have to be to not hear city noises? The trees, they could muffle things. It might not be far. He wondered if he could walk back to the coffee shop where they'd met Alex in the first place.

What if he'd come out here with Sh'Nae? The custodian said they'd be watching him, but who would be watching? He hadn't seen a single person since he left the room. Nor had he seen any cameras, though to be honest he hadn't been looking.

Where was everyone?

There was a round table with benches around it just outside the door, sitting in the sun. It was warm, but not uncomfortably so, and Ganns sat with his back to the table to put the building behind him and enjoy the peace. There'd not been any since San Pedro.

"There you are, Ganns." Dr. Looman walked up from behind, from the building's front door. Ganns hadn't heard him, but then he'd been listening to the insects, trying to figure them out.

The doctor stood beside Ganns for a second, then put one foot on the bench and crossed his arms. "We need to talk."

"That only makes sense," Ganns said. He sat, waiting for the next sentence, even though he knew what it'd be. He'd known since before

Sh'Nae went to nap that they'd pull him aside. It made sense because he was the one with the questions, the one with the doubt. If there was anything a magician hated, it was doubters.

But what was he going to do about it? What could he do?

The doctor told him that he needed another blood sample, because there were tags in his blood that might indicate bad things, but it wasn't clear. Ganns heard Sh'Nae's voiced telling him to give the damn blood, but his reluctance hadn't faded. Ganns decided to use the opportunity to see how much of the show they'd prepared for, and he asked to see the lab where they did the analysis. To his surprise, the doctor agreed and invited Ganns to follow.

The hallways they walked through looked like most corporate buildings, which is to say that they were austere, with white paint and plain furniture, but unlike government buildings this one did have a plush, emerald carpet. The furniture was simple, framed in dark wood and chrome and cushioned with a pattern which matched the carpet. The pictures were all of heads. White, male heads.

The 2300s didn't look much different from the 2000s.

The doctor veered right toward a wide set of cream double doors with brushed steel push plates, went through, and held the door for Ganns. On the far side, the building became instantly medical, with lots of stainless steel taking over. They walked down a long hallway with doors every ten meters or so, and each door wore a broad glass pane laced with steel wire. Explosion proof windows. There were words on the doors, but Ganns wasn't absorbing those. It was the whole thing, it looked real. It looked real.

They turned again, going through another set of double doors, and entered a remarkably small room, one dressed the same as the rest except for the work bench. It had a stainless-steel top and a variety of racks, tubes, and a few appliances. One Ganns recognized as a centrifuge, but that was all. There was also a chair with big arm rests and a technician in scrubs.

"This is where the analysis is done, Ganns. Karlie here does all of these samples, because they're a little tricky and she knows how to get it done."

Ganns nodded. "Karlie," he said. Karlie nodded back, and Ganns faced the doctor. "Okay." He squinted for a second, then released a small smile. "I was wrong. I admit it."

"Take the chair, then. Karlie will take a few more vials and then we'll take you back to Sh'Nae. I expect Alex is already making plans with her about your next move." Ganns sat in the chair and stretched out his left arm. He'd learned, over the years, that that one was easier.

"Do you know what we're doing next?" Ganns asked, while Karlie put a band of rubber around his bicep and poked at the inside of his elbow.

"No, not me. I'm just a lab tech." She wrapped a thick band of rubber around his left arm, then gave him a hard ball of rubber. "Squeeze and hold," she said.

Ganns nodded while Karlie poked him, and for the first time since they'd taken the little pill back in New Orleans, he began to relax. The place wasn't militant, like he'd imagined it'd be. They didn't lock them in and there weren't guards everywhere. This thing, with the lab, and everything he saw getting there, that was too much for a set. He believed they still had a motive they weren't explaining, but at least some of it had to be true.

"That's it," Karlie said. "I've got what I need. We'll get back to you soon, okay?" She gave Ganns a smile. A genuine smile. Something he hadn't seen since before he'd met Alex. The future isn't very smiley, he thought. "Do you need me to show you how to get back to your room?" Karlie added.

"No, I'm in no hurry. I'll meander, if you don't mind."

"Meander away," she said, returning to her tubes of blood.

They'd told her that her phone wouldn't work here, and they told her why, but when Sh'Nae couldn't sleep she couldn't help but play on it. It came with a game, one where an ogre broke colorful bubbles hanging in patterns over his head by throwing elves. Or hobbits. She didn't know the difference.

While the phone's battery was at 31%, her own was way too full. There'd be no napping.

She'd said that she was going to sleep and gave Ganns a small kiss, something she almost never did, but he looked like he needed it. She knew he was here because of her and not because of Darryl, and that was part of the problem. She didn't want to see Ganns suffer, but he did deserve it. At least a little.

She couldn't let on, but it was all too much. Normally she wouldn't allow anything to get to her, because there were always things. You weren't in control if things (or other people) chose what you did and how you felt. She refused to invest energy in things she had no control over. Like everything that was happening now. She could aim herself at finding Darryl, but after that she had to go with the flow. Even the thing with the liver, whether she got it or Ganns got it, fit into that category. The only thing she had control over was what she did and where she went searching for Darryl. That she would do with vigor.

Turning the phone's screen off, she rolled to her side and stared at the door. There were voices on the other side, both male. One was probably Ganns, and Sh'Nae only wondered a little who the other one was. If it was interesting, if it was necessary, Ganns would be through the door in a shot. He'd bounce on the balls of his heels and his voice would do that tight thing it did.

The door must have been solid, because she couldn't pull out any words. Just voices. She rolled over and faced the other wall.

The thing that ate at her, the burning in the pit of her abdomen she couldn't logic her way out of, was the feeling that Darryl was in over his head this time. She knew better than Ganns, better than anyone, really, that Darryl wasn't stupid, and he wasn't naive. You don't live on the streets of L.A. being naive. But he could be hurt, and when he hurt he turned inward. He shut down. That was why she found him the way she did, providing succor to himself beside a dumpster in one of the fouler San Pedro alleyways. That was good, because he'd been in Wilmington before. He refused to talk about Wilmington, so it must have been bad."

She rolled back over again and, staring at the doorknob, saw it turn. It wasn't Ganns, as she expected. Instead, it was Alex.

"You're awake. I thought you might be."

"Why is that?" Sh'Nae didn't move, but Alex came and leaned against the desk beside the bed.

"I've brought a lot of people here before, you know. Probably more than fifty. Fifty people from different realities, diverse backgrounds, with all degrees of education and faith. The religious ones take it worse than the rest."

"I'm not religious."

"No, you're not. You might believe in a god, but you don't let faith blind you. To me, being blinded by faith qualifies as religion. Ganns is religious, in a way."

"Ganns is an atheist."

"But his faith in all that is right and all this is wrong is his religion. You've seen him say things, and do things, more because of what he believes than what's real, haven't you?"

"Everyone's done that before. We all believe in something."

"Not all of us," she said, forcing a small smile. It was as much of a smile as Alex was capable of, and it sat on the few moments of silence before she continued.

"Great segue, Alex. Why are you doing this?"

"Because it's my job."

"Bullshit. Since you travel time and space, I'm guessing you have no life. No significant other. No kids. People who do that do it for some reason. The military and law enforcement, clergy, EMTs, they all have to do it for something besides the paycheck."

"You give people too much credit. My dad was an enlisted guy in the army, and he said he only did it for a job. He said patriotism is bullshit. I think the same way."

"Still not believing you."

"Okay. You want to move on now? I came to talk more about why you're here. You want to do that instead?"

"I'm here because we're going to find Darryl."

"Yes, but why do they have Darryl?"

Sh'Nae pursed her lips. "I don't know."

"You're about to, but you have to let me finish. Okay?"

"Okay."

———————————

"It starts in a world we'd both recognize, you and me. The year was 1900 and the place is New Orleans. Your history books say it started with Robert Charles, but that's because history books spend little time on the back story. It began with a religious man, a bishop named Henry Turner. Turner made his name in history long before Robert Charles shot a white New Orleans police officer, started a race riot, and all those other things that you'll read about him. You won't read that Charles was an acolyte of Turners, because that wasn't news. Turner had many followers.

"A side point, one critical to my line of work, is that, more often than not, history isn't what really happens. Instead, history is what people think happened. They say that history is written by the victors, but that's myopic. History is written, and rewritten, by the dominant pen. My saying doesn't have the same ring to it, but it's truer. As it was, your world doesn't know what it missed, and my world didn't miss it.

"Or maybe it's the other way around.

"Ganns was taking you and Darryl to learn more about Robert Charles. It was going to be another one of his movies. We'll talk about Robert Charles in a second, but I want to tell you why this is happening first.

"In your world, he's hardly a footnote. Outside of academics, New Orleans history buffs, and black studies majors, almost no one knows about the Robert Charles riots. You couldn't have kept it a bigger secret if you tried. But in my world, Robert Charles is a hero, and he's a hero on both sides of the southern border. Why? Because we found common respect through him. He created our world. Robert Charles is a big deal to us, even if there isn't much to be said about him.

"He was a laborer in New Orleans years before he pulled his pistol, and those years were largely unremarkable. He was a complex man. On one hand, he was well-read, thoughtful, and mostly quiet. On the other hand, he was always armed, always, and he had a history of using his weapons when it thought it appropriate. You could say that he had a rigid vision of right and wrong, and he enforced that, at least as well as a single black man in the south could.

"It's been expressed in print that a bishop of a southern church that Robert contacted was a catalyst, that he fed the beast, but that's inadequate. In your history books, at least the ones that mention Robert Charles, Bishop Turner was something of an underdog hero. In our history books, he was wily and willing to die for his cause, a cause that he managed to pull off by bribing another country. Spain."

"Spain?" Sh'Nae asked. *How does one man bribe a country?*

"Yes, Spain. Let me paint you a picture.

"Backing up a couple years before the riot, the Spanish Navy was hit pretty hard by the Spanish-American War. Decimated, really. That's what Americans and the other Europeans thought. But this was never true, because Spain had plans.

"One of the embarrassments for Spain at the end of the 19th century was how her naval forces, once the greatest in the world, had withered. Because of that, the Spanish were doing something about it, one ship at a time. They built a new fleet, then hid the ships at a port they maintained in West Africa. The fleets they lost, those were a decoy, and the reason they were a decoy was Bishop Turner.

"Bishop Turner had several claims to fame, including being a black man elected to public office directly after the Civil War, but the one we care about was his support for the Back to Africa movement. His word, in the form of a magazine he published, worked its way across the south like kudzu, and through it he found influence. The bishop worked this influence in a manner that no one understood back when he was still alive. His followers sold his magazine, door to door, and his followers gave their pennies up for the Back to Africa movement. Those who could saved their pennies to buy passage to some yet-to-be-determined place. They paid for a dream, and it was said, even in polite company, that a dream was all it was. But that's not true.

"On the surface, the bishop was arranging passage from America to Liberia. He proposed hiring the Spanish, who he said were offering the trip at a low price solely to poke the American government. That sold well among the south's discontented blacks. One of the ships, an off-the-books cousin to the Lepanto, her guns not yet installed, even docked at the Port of New Orleans for "repairs", but it was a ruse. Spain did it to show her customers what they had coming. Spain promised the bishop that there were four ships in total, and that they would use these four ships, in as many trips as was necessary, to ferry all of the bishop's customers back to Africa.

"This was a lie. Spain never intended to ferry anyone. What she saw was a chance to leverage this arrangement to access her old territory and everything inland, using the Mississippi. Enough of a chance that, by the end of 1899, Spain had established trade in Santiago de Cuba under America's watchful eye. What America didn't know was that the Spanish had built a small port outside Cartegena where they could create more warships for their hidden fleet, and they were doing so. Quickly. When the summer of 1900 came around, they had five gunboats and a dozen troop carriers, each filled with Infantería de Marina. That would be plenty, because their only goal initially was to take and keep New Orleans. From there, Spain intended to enlist black America in extending the war they intended to bring to America's shores.

"Regardless how many variations in the multiverse there are of the Robert Charles riots, there are largely just two outcomes—the one from your history and the one from mine.

"In our world, Robert Charles and a friend of his went out for a night on the town, and it ended with Robert shooting a police officer. In each and every world where this occurred, this wasn't happenstance. Robert intended to shoot an officer, a white officer, because those were his instructions from Bishop Turner. It made sense. A black man shooting a white policeman would put the New Orleans whites into a murderous fit, and there were over a thousand blacks in New Orleans that day specifically to get on ships coming in from Spain. Not an even fight, but Bishop Turner believed that God and righteous rage were on his side. To be certain, Bishop Turner published fliers which said that, when the ships came to take them to their new world that everyone had to be wary. White people knew they would be leaving through the Port of New Orleans, and the white people might try to stop them. The stage was set.

"Here's where there's a shift. In your world, the Spanish ships never get to New Orleans. Things happened in Bogota, and only one ship set sail. When it nearly made New Orleans without accompaniment, it turned away. It couldn't do it alone.

"Things played out differently in my world. All the ships made it.

"There were several thousand black men and women living in and around New Orleans back then. They were roughly a third of the population. There were also hundreds from outside the city who came specifically to be led to a better life. As predicted, the white people raged, the blacks raged back, and the fight was on. Without the Spanish, this probably wouldn't have ended well for the blacks, because they were outnumbered, and they couldn't bring the same resources to the fight. The Spanish changed that. They landed in the Port of New Orleans and disembarked their marines, each carrying extra weapons to give to blacks fighting their fight. The Spanish gunships took to shooting into the city, creating havoc. Seeing the black man fight back in waves, with heavy guns in the background, that pushed the battle north.

"But it was just a battle. There weren't more than ten to fifteen thousand people fighting, with twenty times that, black and white, looking on in wonder. You'd think it'd peter out, but it didn't. The violence pulsed once, and the whites, in shock, retreated. Then the Spanish marines led waves of locals against them. Within just a couple days word made it east and west, and black reinforcements from Mississippi and Alabama rolled in. From there, the fight grew, some to the north and west, but mostly to the east.

"So, in your world, there was a riot and a handful of people, some white but mostly black, were killed. The whole thing was over within the year. In my world, the movement grew out from New Orleans. The Spanish sent more troops, landing them in Alabama and both coasts of Florida, and then the French offered aid. They were rebuffed, of course.

I have no idea what they called it back then, but we call it the Uncivil War because it was especially brutal on both sides.

"There's a lot of history after that, as you might imagine, because that was four hundred years ago, but we're in basically the same arrangement we were in ten years after the Uncivil War started. That is, there's two different countries, the Southern United States of America, or SUSA, and the Northern United States of America, or NUSA. The difference is black and white. While every NUSA citizen isn't white, none are black. Our constitution won't allow it. The opposite is true in SUSA. We're friendly now, we can travel back and forth, we can even live and work in each other's countries. We just cannot be citizens. Where the border lies there's this strip of anarchy, a place both countries try to claim. That ribbon of land is filled with angry people denying their very history while surrounded by it. Our military sits on the northern border, and SUSA's military sits on the south. It's a miserable place. The strip thinks it's the dog in this fight, but it's a small, toothless dog.

"Why are we here? Because some people want to collapse all the realities together and some don't. I work for the side of don't. The multiverse is natural and should remain. We have no idea what'll happen if we collapse it. That's this scientist's point of view.

"The people who took Darryl want to collapse the multiverse onto my world, leaving only the SUSA and NUSA. Sam Beckett works for them, and he's the one who gets Darryl to shift. What they don't know is that Sam isn't on their side. Sam wants to collapse the multiverse on your world, with only one USA. There are other players, but changing the multiverse isn't their goal. They're not my mission.

"This is why Darryl is with Beckett and why you're here with me. We're still fighting the Uncivil War."

———————

"So many questions," Sh'Nae said.

"Go ahead."

"Why? If you can shift, why not shift to the world you want and forget the rest? Also, what the hell does Darryl have to do with this?"

"Because people aren't ever happy. It's not enough that I get what I want, I have to make sure that everyone else gets what I want."

"That's pretty cynical of you."

"I'm a nihilist to my core, which helps me identify with the presentists. I don't agree with them, but I see where they're coming from."

"Presentists?"

Alex nodded. "That's the name taken by those who want to collapse the multiverse, regardless which universe they choose. I only told you about the two involved here, but there are hundreds of groups. Maybe thousands. They're all around the world and they all have different goals. Almost every country has an organization like the one I work for, a government entity dedicated to protecting the status quo. We're the largest department in NUSA's government."

"Why do presentists want to collapse the multiverse?"

"They believe there is no past and no future, that there is only the now. That we're conscious of only one reality at a time feeds their belief, and like most people they ignore the things which counter it. The funny thing is that presentists can shift, just like we did, which proves that the multiverse they don't believe in really exists. Rather than change their belief system, they intend to make reality match it."

Sh'Nae didn't answer, but instead shook her head.

"Making reality match our beliefs is common. We all do it, to some degree."

"What happens to all the different pasts?"

"They think the past is just thought, it's all in the head. It's an elegant solution."

"This seems like a lot of energy expended over nothing. No matter who's right, nothing changes."

"Hold onto that thought," Alex said. "This is where Darryl comes in. We have to change gears here. Have you ever thought about people who say they've seen life after death?"

"Not much. People see what they need to."

"Now who's the cynic?" Alex asked, smiling. "I don't, either. The presentists offer that where you go after you die is also in the present, and they claim this is consistent with the first law of thermodynamics. When we die, we're just somewhere else, in another reality, but it's different because it's the only one that the living can't get to. Even naturals can't, unless, of course, they die. They also suppose that the dead can't get back here. Somehow, they've extrapolated this belief into it being the reason they've failed thus far at collapsing the multiverse. They've worked it all up in their little minds that they've done everything correctly except include the reality of the dead. From there, they got to Darryl."

"I still don't get it. Why Darryl?"

"They think he can see the dead because he's in two realities at once. He's on both sides. That would be a first. As far as we know, no one's ever been in two realities at once. It's a crap theory, but then the presentists are fond of crap theories."

"If they're right, and they can collapse the multiverse, that'd bring all the dead back? They want to bring Hell into our world?"

"In a way. The presentists don't believe in religious dogma, especially Christianity. Instead, they ascribe to something akin to the Greek's Hades, a place where all the dead go. Again, it's just another reality."

"And you believe them?"

"No. I don't."

"But you're trying to stop them."

"What I do, it's like law enforcement. And like law enforcement, I don't get to choose my assignments."

Sh'Nae wanted to pursue the line of questioning, but the door opened quickly and a small man with dark hair and a uniform stuck his head in.

"Sorry Alex, but we got a runner. I'm locking you two in for now."

"Go ahead, Daniel. Anyone I know?"

"Maybe. His name is," Daniel looked at the palm of his hand, where he'd written it on the skin, "I think it's Ganns? Weird name."

CHAPTER FOUR

Year: 1900
Location: New Orleans, Louisiana

Holding his head, Darryl lay still on the wooden floor and stared at the two boots hanging maybe two feet up and four feet away from his face. He expected something else, maybe a whooshing sound or the pain of impact or lightning bolts, but there was nothing. One second, he was lying on the back seat of Sam's Lincoln, with Sam explaining how to shift and handing him a small, white pill, and the next he was here lying on this floor, this warm wooden floor, staring at boots.

"Come on Darryl, stand up. The floor can't help you." Looking up from the feet, he saw Sam standing beside a table tugging on something. Then the feet swayed, and Darryl shot up so fast he had to stop for a moment, closing his eyes.

"Keep cool. We're only here for the clothing, these guys aren't using it anymore. We need to look the part to get around." The two feet were connected to the black man, one who stretched across the length of his wooden table and whose lower legs dangled anyway. Sam was in the process of stripping him, there in the middle of the room in the middle of the day. "Get your clothing off and put his on." Sam pointed at another table. "The morgue," he said, "is empty at lunchtime. And go easy now. I warned you. Shifting takes a little getting used to, like earning your sea legs." He pointed down the line of dead. "Quick and get to it, we'll be out of here in a twinkle."

Steadying himself, Darryl stood and looked around. They were in a broad room with a fireplace and several tables. Each of the tables had a body on it. The long fellow next to Sam was half undressed and the corpulent woman past them looked to be wearing rags. Then a short man, nude and made of hair, and finally the latter two. These two could have been brothers, both tallish but otherwise average-looking fellows, home-cut hair and simple duds. The one Darryl was to go to looked to be maybe thirty, with a big forehead and stout chin.

Past the last man there was a broad entrance that went into a twilight room with couches and, apparently, no windows. Lit candles flickered about the room.

Darryl wandered over and poked the fellow in the shoulder, and when that didn't raise a fuss, he touched one cheek. He expected the man's head to jostle some, but it stuck.

Why was he dead? He didn't look like he needed to be dead. Even his color wasn't bad. Darryl had seen more dead than anyone he'd ever known, but this one, this one guy, was the first one he'd touched, and he found himself wondering if the dead felt as right as they usually looked. He pushed on the corpse's shoulder and found the flesh firm. Then he poked its neck slowly, watching the skin recede beneath his finger and remain dimpled when he pulled his hand away. For comparison he tried pushing his own neck, but he couldn't tell if he stayed dimpled.

"We have ten minutes before lunch is over and the owners return. They'll be too drunk to notice naked customers, but not too drunk to notice us standing around." The smile was out of Sam's voice now. "Undress him and put the clothes on."

Swallowing, Darryl quit thinking and just did what Sam said. He slipped out of his own clothes down to his underwear, then pulled almost everything off the man from the feet on up. His shirt and pants were cotton, with the white shirt sweat-stained and dirty. His pants were tied around the waist with a built-in cinch and the socks were itchy wool. Lastly came boots of thin leather with more wear than sole.

"Get your stuff, we'll sink it in the river when we can. Wad it all up inside your blue jeans." Darryl turned toward the dark room, the place he figured would have the front door. It looked like a living room. Instead, Sam went through a nondescript doorway centered on the far wall, and Darryl followed him. There was a back porch there, with some tubs, three battered wood dressers, and a simple whitewashed door. Sam went straight out, and Darryl followed. It turned out to be a back door, as behind them ran a dirt alley facing the back of another building, a broad structure of red brick and green-painted doors. Patchy grass broke through the hard earth and occasional bottles littered the space.

"This way." Sam headed down the street, walking slowly on the street's irregular setts. Darryl could tell by the fresh sun that they were heading east. After ten minutes of walking, he couldn't help himself. "Where are we?" he asked.

"New Orleans," said Sam.

"This..." He looked around. "It's not the same."

"It certainly is. This is St. Andrews, where we spent last night in the parking lot. Same exact street we slept in the other times we were here, too. That's not what we're here to change."

"No!" His own volume surprised him, and Darryl lowered his voice. "No. I've never been here before, and there are no parking lots, no stores." He looked around. "There are no streets," he looked at the ground, "it's bricks. There's no asphalt." He stopped and watched Sam keep walking. "No cars, Sam."

Sam stopped. "Not now, Darryl, and not here. I'll explain later, but today you need to just follow me."

"Before?" Darryl started walking, even while trying to think through the tall man's words.

Sam turned and took Darryl at the shoulder, one in each large hand. He stooped in to speak.

"These aren't friendly parts, and we must be quick. The city is looking for you, even now. Please focus, Darryl. Focus, and follow me. Am I clear?"

Darryl nodded, but mostly because Sam had a hold of him.

"Good. Come on then. As soon as we make Adele, we're golden. Let's stay clear of waterfront, because that's where they're searching. This time, it'll be different."

Darryl followed, and he thought Sam might be right. Maybe. It did feel familiar. The air was warm and thick, smelling the sweet citrus of magnolia. He breathed in deep, letting the floral scents clear his head.

The buildings looked like ornamented cakes to him, each one a stacking of discrete levels defined by balconies, balustrades, and assorted ironworks. The streets were dirty, with smears of animal waste and foul-smelling puddles. He saw horses, he saw chickens, but still, there were no cars.

He followed Sam Beckett, and Sam led with only an occasional look back. They worked a cross-street, then went to an alleyway splattered with trash. Sam stepped around everything, nearly doubling his steps to avoid touching anything wet or rusty, and Darryl followed because it seemed like the thing to do. It was almost a game they were playing now, like his lists and the way Sh'Nae worked through them.

Darryl missed Sh'Nae. He missed Ganns as well, but in a smaller way. In the way you might miss a nice pair of socks. But Sh'Nae felt like warmth to Darryl. Like air. Like clarity. Still, he followed Sam because he didn't know what else to do. Sh'Nae wasn't here.

When they turned onto Adele Street, Sam took to walking at the edge instead of the middle, and they only went a short distance before he stopped. Looking up and down the empty street, Sam motioned Darryl toward a dilapidated facade. The doorway wore a raw wood frame made shiny with wear and the door itself looked like heavy oak.

Sam looked at Darryl, down the street, and then back at Darryl. "Are you going in?" he asked finally.

"Just walk in?"

"Yes, open the door."

"But..."

"Walk in, Darryl." Sam pulled a pocket watch and flipped open its cover. "We're two minutes early and I don't want to hazard an accidental intercession." He turned to face Darryl. "Please, go in.

There's a couch on the righthand side, in front of the window. You can sit there, if you'd like."

Following instructions, Darryl gripped the door handle, pushed the latch down, and slowly shouldered the door open. Inside it was dusky because of the thick curtains hanging over the windows, but some light broke through. Motes floated across the sun rays, making the light lazy, and a layer of dust dulled the hardwood flooring. Darryl stepped past the tall coat rack immediately inside the door and turned right into a simple sitting room with one couch of dark green cloth and ornate wood, a matching chair, and an empty shelf built into the wall opposite the front window. There wasn't a light switch, nor any lamps.

He walked to the couch, but it looked as filthy as everything else. Darryl stood beside it instead. He stood and he waited, even when the voices outside the window started. Then the door opened, and men spilled into the room.

Sam came first, followed by a black man with a shaved head and scars across one cheek. He was carrying a leather satchel. Behind him walked a younger fellow carrying a box large enough for two cakes set side by side. Behind him came a white guy, one younger than Sam but still not young. His hair was long and shaggy on his shoulders and his face was specked with gray nubbins. He struggled with a small trunk in his arms.

"Time?" the one with the satchel asked. Sam pulled out his pocket watch. "Seven hours and 12 minutes. We need to get him down, Belly."

"I know the drill. Cal? You bring the measurements this time?"

The white guy pulled a piece of paper out of his front right pocket and waved it at Belly.

"Get on it, then." Cal took the satchel and the suitcase over to the couch. "Sam, take care of Darryl."

Darryl watched Cal sit, open the trunk, and start unpacking pants and shirts and boots, then open the satchel and start digging around in it. He pulled out a series of blue bottles, each corked, and handed two to Sam, who stepped forward to take it. Then Sam turned to Darryl. "C'mon," he said, quietly. "Follow me."

They went back into the hallway and turned opposite the front door, walking through the shadows to the back of the building. The back of the hallway opened into a broad kitchen, with cupboards, a woodburning stove, a table, and a cot pushed up against the nearest wall. The windows were filthy and strung with webs, but light broke through anyway and made the kitchen better than the other rooms. Darryl didn't feel comfortable yet, but he felt better.

"I know it feels like we just started but shifting takes a lot out of you, and we're going to be up all night. Here's a bottle of water and there's a cot. Please drink and try to relax." Sam guided Darryl by one shoulder over to the cot and stood there. Darryl looked down, then up at Sam. Sam uncorked his own bottle, raised it to Darryl, and took a deep drink. He let a small smile slip and nodded. "It's okay, Darryl. I'm on the winning side." He leaned closer. "I've taken care of you thus far, haven't I?"

Thinking back to the meatloaf, Darryl decided he agreed. Sam had taken care of him. Not in the way Sh'Nae did, but Sam hadn't had a chance yet. Maybe he would?

He sat, holding his own bottle of water. It was a pretty blue glass, glass hard to see through.

"Another thing about shifting is that it'll dry you out. Too much of it can make you sick, even. I know it's done that to me. That's why I need you to drink that water. When you wake up, I'll have more for you, okay?"

"Okay," Darryl said. He was tired. He took a small sip of his own, corked the bottle and set it on the floor, then he stretched out on the cot.

While Darryl was doing this, Sam went to the back door, opened it to look out, then shut it again. He listened to the voices in the other room. They were talking low and it was all very calming, just like when Sam talked to him. But, while his eyes did get heavy, Darryl didn't see sleep coming his way. It was hot, the air was sticky, and things were just too different. He missed the couch in the apartment he shared with Sh'Nae. It was softer than this cot, and the air was cooler. Darryl rolled onto his back, staring at the ceiling. He started counting.

Back out in the front room, Belly had the map out and spread across the floor, with Cal and Wallace both leaning over it. They'd pulled back the draperies, filling the air with sunlight and dust. Sam came in and leaned against one wall.

"We've done this four times," Cal said, his voice itself a complaint.

"Wallace hasn't done it four times, and the rest of us haven't ever got it right." Cal nodded, but demeanor said otherwise. Belly continued. "It's a short trip, Wallace. We have to go from here to Dryade, less than two miles."

"I'm the one who lives here, remember? Save it," Wallace said.

"Again, I want to change the trend. I want to stop failing. Anyone else got a complaint to work through before we touch the details again?" No one else spoke. "Okay. Fleet status, Cal?"

"The first ship docks in five hours, the others are offshore and waiting. The second mission's picket boats went out over the last week and are running a net twenty-five miles east."

"How many in the city right now?"

"About 2,000, confirmed through the Methodist insurgency two days ago."

"Trains, Wallace?"

"On time. Jackson is carrying 200, heavily armed, and Opel's got another 130 of the same. Also, On the river we have three sternwheelers totaling 500."

"And weapons?"

"Rifles, pistols, swords, and dynamite stored at safe houses in a circle surrounding the Saratoga house."

"And that's where we want them?"

"It's the best part of this plan."

"This is for everyone. Are there any changes we need to know about? Anything, no matter how small?" No one spoke.

"Robert Charles got things underway a couple nights ago. The locals, black and white, are restless and things are ready to pop. We're a go on all fronts," Cal said. Belly nodded.

"You're quiet, Sam."

"My job is to bring one of the Darryls, and that's what I did. I don't want to find a fifth one, but if that's what I've got to do, that's what I'll do."

"It's going to happen this time, just like it should."

"Right as rain," repeated Cal.

"To be sure, let's go over what didn't work before. The first time we had all the people here, but our arms were on the Jackson train and it was held up in Mangham. Robert Charles started things that the rioters ended, and we couldn't do shit about it." Belly spat on the floor.

"Why'd the train stop?" Wallace asked.

"There was a fight, someone got shot. They stopped to look for a doctor, but Mangham is small change and there wasn't one. The train lost an hour, then left the guy behind and moved on. By then, we'd missed our window."

"That's when we decided to pack the city ahead of time," Cal added, looking at Sam. Sam nodded.

"Next time in, the Saratoga house burned early on and Robert ran from New Orleans after only shooting the one cop in the leg. There was no riot. We had to let things go. The next time the rioters caught our guy and Robert Charles was hung by a mob. We lost round four to weather, and now we're here."

"Weather? Seriously?" Wallace was shaking his head.

"The Galveston hurricane turned north early and destroyed New Orleans instead of Galveston. Cal barely made it out alive."

"This is weird," Wallace said. "I don't know what to do with any of this information. Does it change what I do? Are things any different from the way I was trained?"

"Don't give up, I think. It's always something different that stops us, not one thing we can't figure out. I think that means we can do this, if we're patient. We have you now as the friend we plug into Robert Charles, and I think that'll help."

Wallace shrugged.

"Florance will be by in," Belly looked to Sam, who had his watch out again.

"Two hours and thirty-three minutes," Sam said.

74

"Two Thirty-three," repeated Belly. "Let's get the clothing altered, get dressed, and get moving. Sam stays with Darryl now and gets him to Dryade tonight. That's where you two will pair up, Wallace." Both Sam and Wallace nodded their concurrence.

After sleeping for a few hours, Darryl awoke wishing for a few more. But Sam came to get him, he knew it was time for something. The sun was up and humidity swam with the heat inside the thick clothes he'd donned at the funeral home. The silent house smelled of sweat and earth.

He inventoried his head, like he always did when he woke up, and found the buzzing absent. His thoughts were clear, as were his memories, and the clarity left him stunned. He'd been here, wherever here was, for a good part of the day and there'd been none of those walls in his head blocking his thoughts. None of that anxiety. It was just clean and clear.

"It's time to head out now, Darryl. Just a few more hours until sundown, and after that you and I can return to find Sh'Nae in New Orleans. Does that sound good?"

"I can see Sh'Nae again?"

"Of course! Now let's get a move on."

They left by the kitchen door, and initially Darryl noticed they were retracing the steps they took there from the river. Sweat was rolling beneath the floppy hat Sam had handed to Darryl before they left the house, and his clothes were staining beneath his arms. The heat was different than it'd been back in San Pedro, but still it felt familiar. He knew the atmosphere. It felt like home.

As they neared the river the rows of shotgun houses gave way to a park, with thick tufts of grass and stout trees, thick limbs, and heavy leaves. Sam turned into the park, and Darryl followed him. At least up until three men stepped out from hiding. Then Darryl froze. The three men strode out from a small copse of trees near the river's edge, and when he saw them, Sam froze as well. The lead man, Belly, raised a pistol.

"Was it you every time, Sam?" Belly asked.

"He couldn't have done the hurricane," said Cal, sarcastically.

Sam shoved both his hands into his front pockets, burying them deeply, but he didn't say a word.

"We're not going home now, and we're not coming back. This is on you." Then Belly fired one round, hitting Sam in the chest. He fell backward, emitting a sharp exhale when the bullet hit him, then he laid still. The three walked up to the fallen Sam until they stood over him, then Belly aimed down at Sam, only a foot or two between the muzzle and Sam's head, and shot again. Darryl froze with the first shot and remained frozen afterward. Without Sam he didn't know where he was or where he was going. Running didn't make sense, but neither did standing still. He turned and started walking away, but he heard the steps coming quickly and he knew. He was still here. He was trapped.

Still, there wasn't a buzz. There should have been.

Darryl turned to face Belly, then Cal. Finally, Wallace walked up. They stared at each other for a few seconds, then Belly rubbed his nose. It was Darryl's first good look at the man he'd seen back at the other house. He was older, probably in his sixties, and his shirt was untucked. His pants were dark and heavy, and his boots were tan. He held something shiny in one hand. A watch.

"We're not going to hurt you, Darryl." Darryl looked back at Sam, his face dripping blood and his hair wet and matted. He didn't take his eyes off Sam when he felt a hand on one of his shoulders.

"How do you know my name? How does everyone know my name?" Darryl kept looking at the body, mostly to keep his eyes away from the shooter's own.

"Sam didn't tell you?" At this Darryl turned to face his interrogator.

"Tell me what? He didn't tell me much at all. Now he's not going to tell me anything, is he?"

"I'm Belly. That's Wallace, and he's Cal."

"I know that much, but that's all. I'm so lost. First, we were in San Pedro. I remember that."

"Then what?"

"Then Houston and Sam and a long drive and we slept in a car." Sam squatted and wrapped his arms around his own shoulders. "I don't know."

"He was wrong, Darryl. We were wrong, too. We thought Sam was with us, trying to make things right, but he wasn't. What he was doing was getting people hurt, maybe getting people killed. He was a bad man, Darryl."

"You're doing what?"

"Making things right."

"Right for who?"

"Everyone."

"Except Sam?"

"Sam wanted to keep things wrong. I knew him, Darryl. More than knew him, I trained him. He was smarter than this."

"This what?" For some reason, Darryl found the questions empowered him, made him more confident.

"We'll tell you everything," Belly paused. "No, we'll tell you enough. I don't like to lie, Darryl. Sam, he couldn't help himself. He'd lie to a mirror."

"None of this is right. Nothing feels right."

Belly leaned in and spoke softly. "I shot Sam to save you, Darryl. He wasn't going to help you; he was using you to get his own way. He knew where the story was going, and he wanted to veer it off on the wrong track. He wouldn't have killed you, but you would have died. He was making sure of that."

Darryl stared Belly in the eyes, looking for something there the way he read eyes back on the street. But there was nothing but flat brown. Nothing at all. He decided to stare at Belly's pistol instead. "I'll go if you'll tell me something."

"I will if I can," Cal said.

Darryl motioned back the way he and Sam had come. They weren't far from the buildings, mostly one or two stories tall, some small, some long and thin, but all rectangular. There wasn't anything tall and no modern conveniences. It looked like a painting, but it was real. "Where are we?" he asked again. He didn't believe the first answer.

"New Orleans. Your question shouldn't be where are we, Darryl. It should be when are we. Now come on, we have to get inside again before this goes south. We have a few hours to go. Cal, go find Florance and tell her we're returning to house number two instead." Then Belly took the lead.

There was a row of houses nearby, their outer skins hard and pale, small windows piercing the walls, but too high for anyone to look out. He went straight for the third one from the right in a row of six or seven, the one with its rear door already ajar, and everyone else followed. Once through the door, Belly slammed it shut behind them.

Outside it'd been hot and humid, but it was nothing like the oppressive swelter inside. There were candles everywhere, dozens of them, each sitting on a plate or a strip of metal or in a bottle burning on the wooden floor. Though he'd seen slit windows on the outside walls, inside it looked as if there were no windows at all. No natural light broke through to where they stood, and the candles failed to break to gloom. Belly led him to a wall clear of candles and motioned for him to sit on the floor, then he disappeared for a few moments and came back with a glass bottle. He popped the cork and handed it to Darryl.

"It's river water. Sip slowly, okay?" He sat on the floor next to Darryl and crossed his legs. "Sam must have said some things, eh? What did he tell you?"

"Nothing. He told me nothing."

"Fine. I'm sorry." Belly fiddled with something between his fingers, and as he adjusted to the light Sam realized that it was the cork. Just a cork.

"Let me ask you this. Since you've been here, have you seen any of your ghosts?"

Darryl shook his head. He hadn't, and now that he realized it he was surprised. He didn't realize these people knew that he saw the dead.

"I believe you," Belly said. "Can you let me know if you do? I'm just curious about this power of yours. It's amazing, you know. I believe in it, and I believe in you." He picked up the water bottle and took a sip. "So? What do you think of old New Orleans?"

Darryl shrugged. "I don't know. Everything made sense when I ran away from Sh'Nae. Nothing has made sense since. I feel different here." Darryl looked around at the candles, ignoring the people walking around the long, nearly empty room. "I feel somewhere."

"What? I couldn't hear you at the end."

"Somewhere. Here I feel like I'm somewhere."

"You had to be somewhere before. We're all somewhere."

"No. I wasn't somewhere before. Back then I was everywhere."

Belly gave Darryl a smile and nod, then got up and left.

Darryl was telling the truth about feeling everywhere, but he was lying about the dead. There were two in this house and one next to the door they came in through. The closest was a man, an emaciated man wearing baggy shorts with tightly curled hair across his chin. Like most of the dead Darryl saw, there was nothing obvious indicated why he'd died. He just had. Sometimes, this time even, Darryl wanted to investigate, but more than ever he had to keep the dead to himself, and that meant trying to ignore them. There were times and places to talk about them, and it was never in front of the bodies. Besides, there were other reasons.

He believed he was in New Orleans now. He could smell it. It didn't look the same, though. That was the part he was comfortable with. Everything else felt wrong.

He'd started the trip with Sh'Nae and Ganns, and found the city with Sam. All three were gone now, with Sam dead by this man Belly. Sh'Nae and Ganns were probably still searching for him in Texas, and that was his fault. Or maybe not. Maybe they'd given up and returned to California. Darryl didn't know.

Maybe Belly knew? Maybe he did, but Darryl wouldn't ask, because Belly was a frightening man. He'd come out of nowhere, Cal and Wallace in tow and walking his long walk, and just shot Sam. Just shot him, with just a few words. That was scariest of all. Darryl couldn't ask Belly questions or tell Belly about the dead. He'd keep it all a secret. He didn't know why secrets helped, or how they made him feel more comfortable, but they did. They gave him an edge over Belly and the other guys. So, he sat. He sat, and he stared at the dead across the room.

As he stared, trying to be somewhere (or somewhen) else, the live people faded off and the dead ones faded in. When it started there was Wallace and a middle-aged guy with thick arms who rarely spoke. He was sitting on the floor nearby, staring at the ceiling, and as he grew thin, thin like Darryl could see through him, he saw the emaciated man get up, his clothing swaying across his bones, and stand. He took a few seconds, but Darryl finally realized the emaciated one was a teenager, his eyes hollow and his fingers like talons. He stood there, shaking his head, and it made Darryl want to get up and run. But to where?

The man, no more than a loose collection of dark bones, smelled like the house. Like dust. He moved as a sleepy spider might, collecting his limbs and stepping off the wall toward the front door. Then he looked over his shoulder and motioned for Darryl to follow.

Of course, Darryl didn't.

The bony one was patient, waiting, looking intermittently over his shoulder and then back at the door. He waved again for Darrel to follow.

"I'm not," Darryl mumbled. That was when he noticed the fat white man standing beside him, looking down. The fellow plopped down beside Darryl, his maneuver full of effort, but also soundless. As Darryl watched, the fat man grew into the room and became solid as well.

"That buck thinks he's helpin', but you has a choice. We can chat and maybe I'll be the one that helps."

Unlike the thin ghost, the way the fat man died was obvious. His neck was crooked and raw, and his head tilted off to one side. His eyes, squinting emeralds peering out from folds of flesh, danced as if they'd never seen a noose.

"How come you're with us? We saw you comin', and we're ready, but you been thin as a ghost. Now you're real as Lawrence there."

Struggling for something intelligent to say, Darryl finally gave in to what he thought. "You're dead," he said. He set the bottle of water down and pointed at the white man's neck. "There."

"We're ready for the bringin'," the man drawled, as if he hadn't heard. "Call us home, son." He clasped onto one of Darryl's knees, making his dead self very real, and leaned in close. His breath smelled of sour meat. "Call us home."

Darryl watched Lawrence, who stood at the edge of the hallway motioning over and over for Darryl to follow. It was the hallway Darryl had come in through. Lawrence wanted to go outside. That sounded better than sitting next to the one with the crooked neck, but he didn't know who he was with or why he was there. He pushed the white man's hand off and stood, bracing himself against the wall. It felt the same here, at least in that he didn't trust anyone. Except maybe Sam, and Sam was gone. Darryl turned and walked toward the door…

…and into…

…Wallace.

"Jeebus!" Wallace shouted. "Where in the Sam Hell did you go to? Hey Belly! Found Darryl!" The man grabbed Darryl by the bicep. "We need to talk, son. Not here, not now, but we need to talk. Don't forget. I'm about to be busy."

"Who are you people?" Darryl asked.

"I'm Wallace, and we need to talk." He was insistent. "Not now, though. Don't forget, okay? I'm about to be busy." He backed up a step and started speaking in a normal voice. "Where you've been? We thought you up and left."

"I did leave," Darryl said, just as loud. His intuition said it was the right thing to do. He looked around, saw he was in the same room he'd been in, but the fat man with the broken neck was gone. So was Lawrence.

"Where to?" Wallace asked.

"To the dead, I think. I went to talk to the dead."

"You always see the dead. That's your deal, right?" Darryl just stared at Wallace.

"When you saw the dead, did you go away? Before this time?" Wallace appeared nervous, looking around. Darryl wondered who he was looking for. Then he thought back to Sh'Nae, who was always there for him.

"No."

"A few minutes ago you said you weren't seeing the dead. What changed?"

"I don't know. They showed up. They were moving."

There were noises in the hallway leading to the other end of the house. Voices.

"What did you see?" Wallace persisted.

"I don't know. They moved. They've never moved before. One of them spoke, and he touched me. His breath was awful."

"Shit," Wallace said. "That's a new wrinkle."

"Wallace!" It was Belly.

"Remember, we talking." He gave the shush sign to Darryl, then turned and yelled down the hallway. "He's here, man. Back room again."

"Why!" Belly bustled into the room, straight toward Darryl's face. "Why," he asked again, lower this time, "do you do this?"

"This what?" Darryl looked for the closest wall, then stepped to put his back against it. He started rocking, from one foot to the other and back again. "Nothing."

"He doesn't know, Belly. Okay? He just doesn't know." Wallace stepped between Belly and Darryl, his chin up and his eyes square. Belly looked over Wallace's shoulder, but didn't move otherwise. "Are you messing, Darryl?"

Darryl shook his head. He didn't know what to say. Tapping his forehead, Darryl ignored the question. He didn't know what else to do.

"Seventeen minutes," came Cal's voice from elsewhere in the house.

"We don't have time for this shit." Belly said, walking off.

Wallace looked over his shoulder at Darryl and winked.

"Set," a voice came back.

"We're on, Darryl." Wallace said taking Darryl by the hand. "We're going to make things right this time. And we're gonna talk."

———————————

There was a clang outside, a cowbell sound, and Belly hurried them out. Cal went first, followed by Wallace and Darryl hand in hand, then

Belly came last. They went in a stream to the vehicle, a simple open cart drawn by two donkeys and managed by a woman with bronze skin, a tall red tignon, and her peasant blouse off the shoulders. She kept her eyes straight ahead.

"Dryades," Belly said, and the donkeys yanked them forward. Darryl watched New Orleans pass by slowly, its long, thin houses separated by bare patches of earth, occasional puddles, and tufts of the greenest grass. Everything smelled like home to him, like a place he'd snuggle down. It carried a familiarity and comfort he'd never known in San Pedro, or any of the other places Ganns took him.

Some parts of it made him uncomfortable, like the ill-defined road. But others, like the rhythmic creaking of the wagon wheels and the inline houses with symmetrical doors and windows, were calming. The mostly-dirt yards played out between them, with occasional ruts wandering through. Some grew flowers out front or had chickens (cooped and running free) on their patch of lawn. One house made uneven boxes for greens and tomatoes out of red bricks crusted with mortar. The spaces between the houses revealed what was past them, which was simply another row of houses, another line of dirt, and another row beyond that.

"Why so quiet?" Cal asked himself, but Darryl answered. "The heat." He wondered how he would know, but he just did.

There were a few folks outside, but mostly they kept to their porches. Some in front and some behind. The sun waned and the thick air cooled. The puddles It'd rained earlier, as indicated by the indiscriminate puddles. The air was thick.

Darryl leaned back, his eyes closed, and inhaled the familiarity.

"You and me, we're going to set some things up tonight, Darryl. It's in the cards." It was Wallace talking now, Darryl could tell by his voice. It was higher than everyone else's, and smooth. Wallace could carry a tune, Darryl imagined.

He didn't know why he'd want to set things up, but neither did he disagree. If that was the way this was all to flow, then so be it. It all felt the way things should feel. There was no anxiety, no confusion, and no humming in his head. For once, he felt linear.

Wallace continued. "This place isn't like where you came from, but I think you know that. The times here, they're different. For that, I need you to carry something for me." He tapped one of Darryl's knees.

Down low, below the top of the sideboard, Wallace held a large revolver in his two hands. The grip lay in one and both the barrel and the cylinder were nestled in the other.

"Do you recognize it?" Wallace asked, and Darryl didn't answer. He didn't answer because, in his mind's eye, he did. *I don't like guns*, he thought, but this one wasn't a new thing, nor a frightening thing, to him. He took the revolver by the grip, muzzle down, and bounced it against this palm.

It was right.

"I thought you might." Wallace leaned back and watched the road go by slowly. "We'll be where we're going in a few, and it goes a bit slow after that. Slide that into your right front pocket. You'll find it's deep enough."

Darryl did as he was told.

The wagon turned off of the road onto another, one which looked more or less the same, but apparently it wasn't, because the woman leaned back and said "Dryades" over her shoulder.

"We've got maybe two minutes, then when I signal you and I are going to just slide out of the back of the wagon, okay? She'll slow it down some, but it won't stop. Then we'll go to the side of the road and keep walking. Got that?"

"Got it," Darryl said. When he was with Sh'Nae and Ganns, he knew most of what was happening. It felt comfortable, like he was watching a movie he'd seen before. When he lit out on his own things were strange, but finding Sam made it all right again. Now, with Wallace, it felt right again.

The wagon slowed perceptibly, and Wallace tapped his shoulder. "Let's move," he said, sliding out. Darryl followed. They both turned immediately and walked to the side of the road, watching the wagon slowly pull away. At the next cross street, the wagon turned left, and after a few moments, Darryl could only hear it.

It was just him and Wallace now, walking. The revolver swung in his baggy pocket, and for the first time in his scattered memory, he felt truly free.

They'd only walked a couple blocks when Wallace slowed to point at a house, one shotgun home like all the others. It had a small porch, a sagging screen, and though the windows were open the curtains were drawn. Wallace led them onto the porch and inside.

Inside the house it was sweltering, but to Darryl's surprise it also smelled wonderful. The air was pungent with garlic and paprika, and there was soft humming coming from somewhere to the rear of the building.

"Countess?" Wallace said in a middling volume. The humming ceased, followed by quick footsteps. In just a couple seconds a small woman came through the next room with her arms wide. Wallace caught her in a deep hug, his face broken wide with a smile. Darryl stood, hands at his side, and waited.

"Love, this is Darryl Green. Darryl, this is my wife, Countess." The woman, wearing a long linen dress tight at the shoulders and waist, but otherwise loose down to the floor, smiled at Darryl and gave him a deep head nod. "Good afternoon, Mr. Green." She turned to her husband and raised one eyebrow. He nodded in reply.

Darryl nodded back, then looked around. "Very nice house, ma'am." The sparse front room that greeted them held a small couch and an overstuffed chair, plus some pictures on the wall. It was plain, but clean.

"Thank you, and please come in. It's almost dinner time and I've made us rice and gravy."

"The best! Please dish us up some, when it's ready. Darryl and I have some business to talk to." Wallace took off his hat and waved at Darryl to remove his, which Darryl did, handing it to his new friend. Wallace hung the hats on hooks beside the front door, sat in the chair, and waved Darryl to the couch.

"Surprised that I live here?"

"Can't be, because I don't know what to expect anymore."

"It's about time you got an explanation, then. I don't suppose Sam told you much?"

Darryl shook his head. "To be honest, I don't know what he told me. I was confused when I first met Sam, and I've mostly been that way since."

"Mostly?" Wallace leaned back and crossed his legs.

"It's not the same. I'm not the same. Not as I was."

"Not to be a pain, but I don't know what you mean."

"My thoughts worked oddly before I came here. There were, well, it was like they were in the wind. I had to hang on to them tightly. That usually meant I couldn't think about more than one thing at a time, and even then something might come along and force itself on me. When there were too many, it overwhelmed me. I couldn't think at all. Everything was noise."

"That's changed? Good." Wallace nodded. "Part of me wants to tell you that the reason things are getting clearer is because of me, because I have that kind of influence on you, but that'd be a lie. I don't think it's who you're around, I think it's where you are."

"I don't understand." Darryl smirked for a second, then added "I always say that. Everywhere. All the time."

"Welcome to the party, but it's not a fun one. This party has been making my head hurt for months because I've spent months learning it. You don't have months. You have," he looked at the closed curtain and the waning sunlight showing through, "hours. You only have hours. We can eat, but then we have to be on the street."

"Sure."

"Good. Let's see. What's enough?" He put his hands together, fingertip to fingertip, and stared at the ceiling. "Tell me what the first thing you remember is, Darryl."

Darryl sat silent for nearly a minute, his eyes sometimes open and sometimes not. Finally, he cocked his head toward Wallace and said "it was summertime, in Wilmington. The weather was warm, and people were staring at my clothing."

"Were you a child then?"

"No, this was just some years ago. Four? Five or six? Maybe."

"Do you remember being a child? You had to be a child."

"Of course." He knitted his brow. "Of course, I was a child. But no, I don't remember anything about that. There was the street, then Sh'Nae, and then Ganns."

"See, I remember you when you were a child. Now, this is where we talk about secrets, okay? This group we're with? Me and Cal and Belly? All the rest? There are many more. We're all full of secrets. For example, they all know that I lived in New Orleans when they recruited me, and that you lived in New Orleans, too. They don't know about this house, though. And they don't know that you and I grew up together in Mississippi. They think you're younger than you are, but you're in your mid-forties. All this stuff, even if they knew, wouldn't matter to them. It wouldn't change anything. They don't care about you because of who you are, they only care about you because of who you were. They're using you." He paused for a second, staring at the ceiling. "They're using both of us."

Wallace sat up and put his elbows on his knees. He stretched his neck forward.

"I care about you because you're my best friend. You've always been my best friend. I know what's supposed to happen. Again. And it'll break my heart. Again." He stood up and started pacing.

"What's that?"

"This is my second time through this year, and last time you died. I wish I'd been with you, because maybe I could have changed things, but I wasn't. You were with some young thug and started shooting cops. The whole town went crazy, as I expect it's doing right now, and you take them all on from a house a few blocks from here. You get shot, and you start dying, but you never finish dying. That's what they think."

Darryl stared at Wallace, processing what he said, but he couldn't. He couldn't imagine he might be one of the dead. "What do you think?" he asked.

"I think they believe you're supposed to get halfway to dying again tonight. Halfway, that's the key to them. It's ridiculous." He sat again, rubbing his head, then quit and looked at Darryl.

"In the month of July, the year 1900, there was a riot in New Orleans. Some asshole police harassed a man, you, and you fought back. For four days, you went about delivering vengeance, but it didn't work out for everyone. Nearly thirty people died and many more were injured."

"Four days, and then I died?" Darryl asked.

"Halfway. Only halfway."

"Did I use this?" He patted the revolver in his pocket.

"Some. But you mostly used a Winchester rifle. I don't know where that's at, but I expect before the night's over you're going to find it."

Darryl waited for Wallace to continue.

"Today is Friday, July 27th. The year is 1900."

Darryl stared at Wallace, not taking his eyes off, not flinching. He expected something, but not that.

"What I don't understand is how this works with two of you here, Robert. You just got here, but if things are on schedule you started shooting three days ago. If that's you shooting, then how are you hear with me? And how do *you* get that rifle in your hand, when the other you is already holding it? I've asked before, but Belly won't tell me. It's another one of their secrets."

Darryl paused for a few seconds, then said "you just called me Robert."

"Because that's your name. I don't know who Darryl Green is. You're Robert Charles. I've known you as Robert Charles for over forty years.

"Don't think about it too much, okay? First off, you're here. There's another one of you here, too, and I guess you're both my friends. I don't know. That's the complicated thing, because unless you two are in the same place doing the same thing at the same time, this ends more than one way, no matter what we do. That's what I think happens. The others don't see it this way because they only see what they want, but it's true. It has to be true.

"I'd tell you that the reason I'm here is to save you, but until these guys, Belly and the rest, came to me, I didn't know you needed saving. I would have gone on through this day, probably fishing like I usually do. Maybe I would have been caught up in the riot, but I don't know because I've never been there before. These others, they have. What they're looking for is a specific outcome, one which hasn't occurred yet. They think you can help them get there. Maybe. But that outcome might also kill you."

"I don't want me to die either," Darryl said.

"Good, we're thinking alike. There's another thing, something they believe, that I don't want to be part of. I don't think you'll want to be, either. The reason why there are several versions of this day where you didn't die is because time doesn't work the way we think it does. This part I know to be true, because I left a few days ago, but I was gone for months. Best way I can explain it is that right now can be all times, anywhere and everywhere, all at once."

"Don't think about it too much." Wallace paused. "We have to be careful," he finished. "They told me what happened tonight last time, and they told me what they want out of all this if it goes according to their plans, but I don't know what does happen. They're trying to arrange the future, but they really don't either. I thought an answer would come to me by now, that I'd know what to do, but I don't. I can hide you, but they'll find us, and they'll shoot me, just like they shot Sam."

"Was Sam helping you guys? I thought you were all together."

"There are many sides to this. I can't keep track. He was part of our team, but he wasn't doing what he was s'pose to. I think Belly thinks he was a spy or that he was sabotaging the mission, but I don't know why. There's just too damn much that I don't know!"

"I wonder why I'm supposed to almost, but not quite, die."

"Yeah, that" he said, waving at the front door. "It's about the dead people out there. The ones you see."

"Okay, keep going," Darryl urged. Wallace stood, crossing his arms just a few feet from Darryl, and stared down at him.

"They believe they can bring all of time and space together, in one time and one place. One world. They believe they would have done this by now if it hadn't been for dead. Belly and Cal and Sam all could travel between worlds, and they taught me to do it, too. But none of them can get to the world of the dead, and they think that's why they're failing. That once they can get to all worlds, they can make them one. When they heard of you, they decided you can get there. You can break down their last barrier."

"How do I do that?"

"That's the question, isn't it? Tell me, do you see any dead people in here?"

"I've only been in this one room," he said, looking at the doorway. He could hear Countess singing to herself somewhere deeper in the house.

"But are there any?"

"No, there aren't any in here."

"Good." He took a deep breath. "I needed to know that."

"Belly can travel between worlds?"

"Yeah, it's called shifting, and Belly can do it without trying. Sam could, as well. Me and Cal take a pill to make it work. I went away from here once, to go get trained, then I came back with more pills in my pocket, but Belly believes you don't need the pill. He called you something, some kind of nickname, but I can't remember what. He also thinks that's how you ended up seeing the dead. He says you shifted just as you were dying, and somehow that left you trapped in this world and in that world at the same time. That's why you're special. There are many, many people who can travel between worlds, but they don't know of anyone who's ever been in more than one world at a time."

"Is that true? Am I in more than one world?"

"I don't know. Have you got a better answer?"

"No, but I think I've always seen the dead."

"You haven't, and I'll guarantee that. We grew up together, and you were afraid of ghosts like no one's business. It's funny, because you weren't afraid of anything else. Not adults, not white people, not books, nothing. But you were afraid of ghosts."

"Did you know me here in New Orleans?"

"We went crawdaddin' in June, if that's what you mean. Just a month ago."

"You and me, we went crawdaddin' last month?" Darryl didn't know what crawdaddin' was.

Wallace nodded.

"What's crawdaddin'?"

"Never mind." He paused. "I know you're you, but you're another you. Lookin' the same, tall and all, but you didn't go by Darryl. You went by Robert. You were thicker, too. Now you look sickly."

"What's crawdaddin'?"

"It's catching bugs from the water to eat. They're like small lobsters."

"You eat bugs? Did I eat bugs?"

Wallace stood still, rubbing at one eye. "Never mind," he said. "Forget the bugs. Where were you in June, Darryl?"

"We were touring in support of our last movie."

"I don't know what a movie is."

Darryl stared at him.

"We've still got a couple hours. The other Robert's got to be hiding out somewhere, but we can go to his place on 4th and his Clio watering hole. Can't hurt to try."

Darryl looked at the doorway that led back to the kitchen.

"You're hungry. Crap. Sure, let's eat quick, then we'll go. Countess!!"

Darryl nodded.

———————

After Darryl scarfed two full bowls of rice and gravy, Wallace led him on a quick, straight-line tour of the neighborhood between Wallace's house and their destination. The roads were still hardpack here, but Wallace rambled on about how where they were going had plenty of roads bricked in. Just not on this end of town. As they walked, some of the shotgun houses gave way tall, thin buildings with wrought iron railings on their upper balconies. In other places there were fields patched with autumn sage, phlox, and plenty of blue-eyed grass. Darryl sweltered inside the scratchy clothing, but he tried not minding it. He tested one pants pocket edge between two fingers, finding it thick and unyielding. His first thought was that he'd never worn anything like these, but that couldn't be true. If Wallace was right, he'd worn plenty. Darryl couldn't decide if what he heard made sense, but it certainly fit with everything else that happened since he'd run from Sh'Nae and Ganns. It certainly looked like he'd traveled back in time, and was time travel any stranger than seeing the dead lying about? Or the dead talking nose to nose with him?

Darryl thought backwards as he walked, starting with his running away. Back to the apartment, and their last question and answer period after the Okinawa movie played. Before that, there were days of blur where he sat on the couch, stood beside the couch, sprawled on his bed, or stood on the balcony. They made movies. They traveled. He answered questions.

Before that, there were streets. Alleys. Cubbyholes and parks. Wet or dry, hot or cold. The smell of the ocean on the fog.

All through his memories, the dead spotted the streets, the hallways, and the beaches. Everywhere there, and everywhere here. They'd passed four since they left Wallace's house, one of which was trying to dig himself out of the soil beside a house. That one paused and waved to Darryl, and Darryl fought the urge to wave back.

They'd walked at least a mile of Dryades Street and taken a quick jog over to Baronne Street when Wallace stopped and cocked his head. There was the body of a young boy, probably not four years old, lying alongside the road probably fifteen yards ahead, and for a second Darryl wondered if Wallace was beginning to see them. That wasn't it though, because Wallace wasn't looking at the boy.

"Do you hear that?" he asked.

Darryl closed his eyes and listened, and he did. He did hear it.

A swell of voices rose from the north, some talking and some yelling, and the whole of it pulsed in a series of quick waves.

"The riots shouldn't have made it over here yet. It's too early." They sped up until they came to the next cross street, where they saw a crowd of white people walking down Josephine Street, heading their direction. "Way too early. Quick, over there." Wallace pointed at one of the tall houses, one right on the cross street, and jogged toward its porch. "C'mon," he insisted. Darryl followed, but at a walk. Wallace was already beating on the door as Darryl approached and the door cracked open. Wallace explained something in a low voice, pointing back at the street, the doorway widened, and Wallace stepped in. He motioned Darryl to hurry after.

Inside they were greeted by a squat woman, her hair trimmed close to the flesh and her pendulous earlobes weighed down by thick, silver hoop earrings. She wore a simple dress of thin cotton which roiled as she walked with her deceptively light step. After shutting the door and twisting the lock, she dropped a steel bar across it and pinned the bar in place. Then she motioned for them to wait and walked toward the back of the building, where she made similar noises at what was probably a back door.

"Let's go upstairs. We can watch safely from there." Darryl followed her, looking around as he went. Outside there'd been windows covered with curtains, but inside he saw wood nailed up over them, and the room was lit with dull metal oil lamps. She grabbed the one nearest the first step and walked straight up, with Darryl following and Wallace in the rear.

Upstairs was much lighter, as the windows weren't covered. The windows were open and, though there hadn't been a breeze and it felt just as hot, the air was fresher. The woman walked between a broad bed and over out onto the balcony and motioned for Darryl and Wallace to follow.

"We'll be seen out there," Darryl said.

"It's okay, honey. White folk are lazy. They'll string you up in the street, but they ain't using no stairs. If I'm wrong, we can come back inside."

The voices grew louder, and a few of the pack's leaders were standing on Josephine Street just before it met Baronne, looking left and right, but not up. One of them carried a smooth piece of wood, like an ax handle, and the other stood with one hand at his side and the other scruffing his whiskers.

"I'm Wallace and he's Darryl. Thanks for letting us in."

"Antonia, but you can call me Tony. It ain't nothing."

Darryl walked past Wallace and Tony to the edge of the balcony closest to Josephine Street, so he could see down a ways. The rioters were strung out in small groups and moving slow, but they were yelling at each other, and a few were pointing. Some carried sticks, some rifles, and some ropes. Some frowned and some laughed, but they all looked evil.

"They don't need to get through the door," Darryl said. "They can just shoot us."

"Not going to happen, child. We're just some dumb niggers watching up here and we're not the problem. Niggers free on the street, they're the problem. They're after someones, right? If they think they've found them someones, it'll get bad."

"Bad," Wallace repeated.

"Yeah, it'll get bad. Just keep quiet and watch. They'll pay us no mind."

Darryl leaned against the wall and watched the milling about, their voices first nibbling on his focus, then chewing on it. If he felt this way back home, he'd think the buzzing was next, but the buzzing didn't happen here. His brain remained straight and his thoughts, while crowded, were clear. The anger scared him, regardless Tony's confidence. He also wondered how Wallace could believe that he was the same guy who Wallace grew up with, because how could he get that thought out of his brain? Then he thought I'm here, in past New Orleans. That's how.

He jumped when someone shot a rifle, but on looking down he couldn't see any of the rioters aiming theirs. The muzzles were mostly pointed at the ground or lying lazily across a shoulder. Wallace had taken a step closer to the doorway into the house, but Tony was still leaning against the balcony rail and looking down, her face passive. He wondered if she knew fear at all.

In a window of relative quiet, Darryl heard something else, a faint sound that felt like the emerged from his own head.

"This might ruin everything they planned," Wallace was saying to no one in particular. "Everything." Tony wasn't listening to him, and while Darryl heard him, he had his head elsewhere. "So much for mission number five. They're not supposed to be here yet!"

It was a thrum, really. A swish and a thrum. Darryl tried focusing on it, but the noise was light and airy, like a whiff of something carried away quickly on the wind. He looked down and saw that there was a knot of three white men staring up at them. Two of them had their hands free, but the one in back had a long rifle held in his crossed arms. They should have kept Darryl's attention, but it wasn't working. He slid back to the swish and the thrum. The swish and the thrum. The swish and the thrum.

Below him the bulk of the white people moved into the street crossing, and there were probably fifty of them. He looked down, then up Josephine Street, then back over his shoulder.

Then he knew where the noise came from.

Probably three blocks down, he saw the dead walking toward the angry white men. There were scores of them, some dragging gimpy legs, others sagging left or right, their skin all sallow and dull. Unlike the group beneath them, Darryl saw the dead were mixed. Besides blacks and whites, there were Asians and Mexicans and Indians. There were as many women as men, maybe even more, and their ages ran the gamut.

So many dead.

Though they were heading straight for the rioters, they didn't look militant. Instead, they looked happy. They looked celebratory.

The sound came from their attempt to march in unison. No one was calling cadence, but they were trying to keep their footsteps left— right—left. As he watched, Darryl saw the swish of those dragging their limbs and the thrum of setting them down.

He looked left and right, seeing the distance between the two crowds. There were just a few blocks before they met. *They won't meet*, he thought. *Because I've not been shot yet.*

"This isn't right," Darryl said.

"That's what I was saying," Wallace said. "We're off, or they're off. Something is off, and Belly isn't here to make the call. Shit."

"Calm, boys. Stay calm. They'll pass. See?" She pointed at the crowd as the bulk of it moved through the intersection down Josephine. Darryl watched them, noticing that not one seemed to see that they were moving headfirst into a platoon of the dead. After looking left and right again, at both crowds, he decided he couldn't wait any longer. "I've got to go," he said. This drew Tony's attention, and she shook her head. "You're stayin' here, boy."

Darryl walked swiftly past her and Wallace and headed down the stairs. He couldn't go out the front, but there was no reason to not go out the back door and back west, the way they'd come. He heard Wallace behind him, so he bolted, making the door three steps at a time. He skidded to a stop, pushed open the bar and unlocked the bolt, then stepped outside.

Darryl turned right, between the buildings, and continued away from the point where he was sure the dead would meet the living. He didn't want to watch it and didn't want to hear it. The voices were still there, the white rioters, but the sound of the dead walking was gone now. He dodged left, between houses, across the next street, and moved further west. At this point, he was no longer interested in where he was. He was only interested in where he wasn't.

This feels familiar, he thought as he ran. He'd done it in California before, more than a few times, when he was walking Avalon Boulevard at night and cholos chased him. There he'd been afraid, worried about what they'd do to him, but it wasn't like that now. Instead of running scared, he was running to make a difference. To change an outcome. He knew, intuitively, that his not staying there kept the dead and the living apart, and for some reason that was important.

After a series of turns, he found a space between houses, in the middle of the block, where he could squat and lean against the wall to catch his breath. There were noises still, he heard individual voices and somewhere there were chickens clucking. The air was moving now, too. The moisture grew heavier, and he smelled rain.

He paused and listened, and there was no swish—thrum. For a moment that made him happy, but then he thought of Wallace. He'd lost Wallace, and now there was no one to help him.

96

CHAPTER FIVE

Year: 2317
Location: Near Chicago, Illinois

They said it was the year twenty-three something, so where were the flying cars? Ganns walked through the trees, pausing on occasion to look behind. Karlie was right, he could just meander away.

The building he was leaving behind was a two story, red brick number with white trim that might fit in almost any city across the country. The grass was a little long, but it was neat and framed by dark timbers cut to fit an angular frame. The edges were flowered, but with what kind Ganns had no idea. The forest had trees with broad leaves, and they'd make good cover if they were closer to the ground. But they weren't. There were bushes, thin and scraggly bushes, as well as grasses and ivy. Looking up, Ganns saw there wasn't much sun getting through the canopy, forcing the little plants to live in shadows.

Then it'd be shadows for him as well.

They might have let him escape. Released him on purpose. So far, it didn't appear that they were after him. There were no alarms sounding and no lights blinking, nor could Ganns hear any cars. There were just insects and the occasional bird. He continued walking, trying his best to stay in a straight line. There had to be a road close by. When he found it, he'd follow it. Somewhere.

On the other hand, they could be watching him. There could be cameras in the trees. He might've been bugged after he took their little white pill. Ganns checked his pockets but didn't find any surprises.

A sizable chunk of Ganns regretted leaving Sh'Nae behind, but it made her safer. Something told him that he was the crux of this ruse, and it likely had to do with money. Everything else in the world did. His leading them off didn't change that, but maybe his stressing their plan would reveal a kink in it, something that Sh'Nae would see and then understand. Otherwise, when they found him, they'd tell him he'd tested positive for that liver thing. When Sh'Nae heard that, she'd freak out and do whatever they asked to ensure his safety. Ganns didn't need that.

After probably twenty minutes of walking (albeit slowly) through the woods, he came across a road, but it wasn't what he'd expected. It was less than five feet wide of thin asphalt, with no painted lines indicating lanes. It looked more like a walking path than anything.

Deciding it was likely a maintenance path for the institution, Ganns crossed over it and into the woods on the far side.

He walked another ten minutes and found he'd have to change directions if he wanted to keep walking. Ahead of him was a shoreline, ostensibly that of Lake Michigan, and he found himself staring at a vast expanse of rippling blue water. To the right the water went to the horizon, but to the left he found another shoreline only a few miles away. He couldn't see the Chicago skyline, which meant they'd probably lied to him. Lied to him, or he was on the wrong side of the island. Part of him wanted to believe if he walked the shoreline he'd eventually see the New Orleans skyline, but this didn't smell like seawater and it didn't look like the muddy Mississippi.

He looked over his shoulder. He could head back. He might be able to find the facility. Then he could skirt it and find out what the opposite direction led to. But no. There was a good chance the facility had people out looking for him. Getting caught wouldn't help Sh'Nae at all.

The next option would be to turn right. It appealed to him, mostly because he had no idea where turning right would lead. Turning left would mean following the shore in the direction of a far shore, one that might be one state or might be the other. Could he tell them apart? He had no idea.

He could fall back to the road and flow alongside it. It differed from his other options by offering the potential for intel. He could see what traffic there was, and maybe that would provide information. Again, he could take the road toward the facility or toward the unknown, and again he had to choose between maybe running into guards or wandering blindly.

Ganns chose the road, deciding to decide when he got there.

Gary torqued the wheel back on the cart with the impact wrench, then set it aside and looked around the front of the cart toward the other side of the shop. Butrus was still sitting there and still playing with his ratchet, spinning it over and over on some randomly selected Stanley deep socket. Butrus loved the sound, but it left Gary shaking his head.

They'd nursed this work cart about as far as they could, and he'd told the superintendent more times than he could count, but did the superintendent listen? Fuck no. The tires were dry-rotted and only worked because of inner tubes, the brake pads were in the rivets, and one of the front A arms was bent, no doubt from a short battle with a pothole. They could afford a new cryogenics lab, but not a goddamned utility cart. Goddamned government and their piece of shit cart. Goddamned piece of shit cart and the goddamned piece of shit company which owned it and the goddamned piece of goddamn shit research facility on this lonely piece of shit island.

Gary checked the torques one more time, then released the bottle jack and dropped the cart to the hardpacked earth of the shop floor. The bastards wouldn't even pay for a concrete floor, which meant not ever using a jack in the wintertime unless the earth was frozen.

Goddamned government.

"Ready?" he called out to Butrus, but Butrus didn't hear him.

He was still playing with his socket.

"BUTRUS!" The boy looked up, giving Gary a sheepish grin. "You ready, boy?" Butrus nodded and stood, bringing his entire 325-pound frame to bear. Fat pushing up over the braces of his overalls and stretching the bib to its limit. "Sit on the tail, son," Gary said, pointing at the back of the cart. He didn't want Butrus to join him, but he needed him to for a couple reasons. First off, he needed to have some weight on the cart to see if the used hub he found was true. A loaded cart would reveal that instantly. Secondly, Dr. Pacione foisted off his son on Gary for a reason, and Gary knew it. He was getting paid more for his daycare capabilities than he was for his mechanical skills. But fuck it. Thirty shitty bucks an hour was thirty shitty bucks an hour.

After Butrus sat on the tail and Gary had him scooch back enough to keep from falling off, Gary got in the driver's seat, turned the key, and selected the transmission to "forward". When he stepped on the pedal the electric cart moved slowly, its suspension groaning. They had some room to the load limit, but not much. Maybe another hundred pounds. Plus, these things were never capable of what they advertised.

Pieces of shit.

The suspension groaned as Gary moved out of the driveway and onto the track. He floored the accelerator, mostly because there was no difference between flooring it and tickling it. The cart either went or it didn't. They accelerated up to top speed, in the range of ten miles per hour, and Gary gave the steering wheel a couple jerks left and right. The cart felt sound and, without the resonant hum, he'd obviously fixed the bent hub. Another success story for Gary's Garage and Daycare.

It was early afternoon, and he hadn't had lunch yet. Butrus had already eaten, but then he was always eating, and besides, he got his food for free at the company choke-and-puke. Lunch was a good enough reason to call the cart fixed. He slowed down, did the six-point version of a three-point turn, and headed toward the southside parking lot. Maybe he'd find Cheri there still?

Ganns found he could stay twenty or so yards off the road and still see it clearly, which gave him a chance to hide if he heard something. The good thing about the ground he was walking on was that it was wet and mulchy, therefore quiet. He could sneak.

Of course, so could they.

Ganns walked for twenty minutes along the road until it turned to follow the shoreline. He didn't want to go to the shore because he lost the tree cover, but then there hadn't been any sounds. Not one. He waited a short time, then walked out to the water's edge and the line of riprap bounding it. There wasn't a shore, per se. No sand. No soil. Just large, jagged stones pile atop one another by men. There was nothing natural here. The riprap went as far as he could see.

He walked along the edge for thirty yards, then decided that this meant the chunk of land he was on was manmade. Did that mean anything to him? Should it?

He followed the waterline anyway. It wasn't a trail, per se, but there was an absence of trees and plants, leaving a band of short grasses running above the stones, and it felt parklike. Ganns considered the value of staying beneath the trees instead of following the water, but he noted that, since he'd left the facility, no one showed him any attention. In fact, he'd remained alone the entire time. It didn't make sense, but it was what it was.

He found the coast he followed to be curving left, and he saw the shoreline opposite him growing. After walking fifteen minutes, a city skyline interceded, and then he knew. It was Chicago. Because why wouldn't it be?

Stopping to rub his eyes, Ganns asked himself that question again. Why wouldn't it be?

He could ask himself that a thousand times, and he should be able to come up with a thousand different answers. Why shouldn't it be? He could count the ways, starting with the fact that there was no sane way he'd made his way from Louisiana to Illinois without knowing. That was a good start. Still, it was Chicago. He recognized the twin peaked steps of Willis Tower. It looked like a tall wedding cake.

So maybe they weren't in New Orleans, or Louisiana, anymore. That much was true. But the presence of America's third largest city didn't undo all of Ganns' other suspicions. They had taken a drug to get there, because that's what Alex required. He and Sh'Nae were knocked out for hours and maybe they took a government jet to get here. With influence, that could be done in, what, six hours? Maybe that, if it included the trips to and from the airports. He didn't know how long they'd been out.

He stretched, pulling out the tightness in his muscles all this sudden exercise instigated, then continued walking. By the time he was square on with the city he realized he was on an island, because if this was a peninsula, or if there'd been a bridge, it'd be on this side. He was closest to the mainland here, and the whole island was behind him. Ganns continued his walk, but he knew what he'd find: water and riprap.

No wonder they didn't mind if he wandered around. He wasn't going anywhere.

Of course, everyone on this island had to have a way off of it. There'd be a dock somewhere, or a helipad. The latter was unlikely, as you couldn't shuttle the whole staff by air. There'd be a dock. It wouldn't have any boats, though, because that was how they controlled travel. Ganns looked toward Chicago again. The boat he needed would be over there.

The only way across right now, Ganns suspected, was to swim. Even in the dead of summer, swimming a distance in Lake Michigan would sap you. You'd drown.

I'll just walk the island, Ganns thought. *Walk it and see what I can see.*

As he walked, Ganns reconsidered whether he'd be the one chosen to get the liver thing. They called it NAS. If they were going to do something like that to him, they'd have to have a reason, and the only reason that came to mind was control. They already had control. They had him and Sh'Nae on this island and, if they wanted to, they could ensure that they never got off. Why the manipulation? Where was the benefit? Because they needed either Ganns or Sh'Nae to do something willingly?

That seemed likely.

Not him, though. He had nothing to offer but doubt. What did Sh'Nae bring to table? Darryl was the obvious target, but they said they knew where Darryl was. They knew how to get to him.

Why would they care if Sh'Nae and Ganns were involved at all?

Ganns walked, thinking.

To get Darryl to do whatever it was that Alex was supposed to get him to do, that's what.

It was a chain reaction, with them influencing Ganns to influence Sh'Nae in order to influence Darryl. If only Ganns could figure out what they wanted Darryl for, this might make more sense. He might be able to put it all together.

He followed the amazingly symmetrical shoreline for another thirty minutes, slowly picking his steps and watching the water. The sun glinted off the water's ripples and trees shushed the mild breeze. It was beautiful. Ganns continued his reverie until he saw the dock he knew he'd find, along with another asphalt path. The dock was wide, probably thirty feet, and it jutted out into the water on pylons for three times that. There were multiple cleats along both sides, and at the end Ganns saw two men sitting with their legs over the edge and their backs to him. There was a utility cart parked on the path where it met the dock, and one of the rear wheels was off and lying on the ground.

He paused, uncertain. The men were talking, their voices low. It looked like they didn't know he was there. He looked around, focusing on the road and the trees near it, but there weren't any signs of a trap. In all honesty, it looked like just two guys sitting on a dock and nothing more. Which, of course, left him wary. He decided there wouldn't be any hiding, but he also wasn't willing to just walk up and shake hands. If they heard him and they wanted to talk, they would. If not, he'd continue around the island.

They heard him.

No more than ten yards past the dock, he heard a "halloo!" and the sound of feet. Turning, he saw a man at a slow jog his direction. He was about six feet tall, with bushy blond hair and a bushier beard. His shoulders were narrow and his gut protruding. There was another fellow behind him, one just trying to stand, who was shorter and broader. Much broader. Ganns cleared his head and waited until the jogging guy was close enough to talk to.

"Morning!"

"Afternoon's more like it. You lost, mister?"

"No," Ganns thought quickly. "I told them I like to exercise, and they said I could take a hike."

"Oh, that sounds like them. Yeah."

"Looks like your cart is broke."

"Again. We're not in any hurry to fix it, though. It's a pretty afternoon. Not too hot." His voice trailed off.

"Don't worry, boys. I didn't see you."

"It's okay. They don't care where we're at or what we do, just as long as I stay with Butrus," he waved back at the obese man still trying to walk up the dock, "until it's time to clock out."

Ganns looked over at the approaching Butrus. "He's with one of the bosses, eh?"

"How'd you guess?"

"Just lucky. It's good of you to watch over him like that. I expect that fellow Butrus probably doesn't have many friends."

The guy nodded. "Yeah. People are pieces of shit. I guess Butrus is okay. He hugs me every day, when he goes home."

"Do you hug him back?"

"Yessir. Kinda have to, of course. The man is silly strong."

"Good on you, son. What's your name?"

"Gary."

"I'm gonna keep walking, Gary. It was good meeting you."

"You too, mister. You heading back to the Titor Center now?"

"No, not yet. Like you said, a pretty day. I'll find it when I'm done hiking."

"It's easy enough. Just head straight away from the waterline toward the center of the island. That's where it's at. You're never far from it. I haven't been far from it in years."

"Are you sad about that?"

"Nope. It just is. God go with, mister."

Ganns nodded. God had to go with someone, he supposed. He turned to leave but found two women in security uniforms only ten feet away. One held something in her hand that looked like a Star Trek phaser.

"Back up, Gary."

"Oh shit. Sorry, mister."

"It's no problem, Gary. I understand."

"I don't, but they didn't give me a choice."

Ganns quit talking and put his hands up on the back of his head. It didn't look like a gun to him, but she was aiming it like one. No doubt it'd do something he didn't like.

"Now what?" he asked.

"Mr. Ganns?"

"Ganns. Just Ganns."

"We need to go back to the center now, Ganns. They don't understand why you ran away. You've concerned them."

"Them who?"

"Management."

"Sure. Management. Management's always concerned, aren't they?" Ganns took two steps forward, then stopped. He couldn't see what he had to lose.

"Will you come with us?" the young lady asked. She nodded back behind her, where Ganns saw a pickup truck. It was rounded at the edges more than any he'd seen before, and if it weren't for the grill announcing "Ford", he'd have no idea where it came from. He looked over his own shoulder, back at the city of Chicago. Yep, still Chicago. Future Fords in an existing city. Some of their story worked out, but he didn't know how much. He still couldn't find trust them.

"Sure. Can I walk back? Gary told me how to get there."

"We'd rather you come back with us," the guard said.

"Are you going to hogtie me?"

"No. We won't even cuff you. You can walk back to the truck, get on the bench between us, and ride back. It's that easy."

"Will you put that away?" Ganns pointed at whatever she was aiming at him.

"When we get there, yes."

Gann's tried to take two more steps forward, but he wasn't paying attention to his feet. On his second step he tipped a rock sticking up out of the earth and shifted forward. Before he hit the ground, he felt his muscles lock up solid as the rock which took him down. He was rigid and unable to catch himself, but he saw it all. He felt it all. He thought through it all. The ground met him hard, and he felt his nose crush. His body shook, and it was like he was watching it all.

"Shit, that was early," a voice said.

"Good job, Billie. Good fucking job."

"I thought he was coming at us. It looked like it. Right? It looked like it?"

"Right. Shit. Let's get him up."

When the energy that took him down waned, something popped into Ganns' head. He was on an island, but he didn't take a boat to get here. At least, not as he remembered it (because he didn't remember a thing). Plus, they were outside Chicago. That much was a fact. He'd been in New Orleans.

When he'd traveled here it was under instruction by Alex. She'd given them their little white pill, one that looked like the cross tops from his school days. Before he and Sh'Nae took them, they were instructed to picture Alex. Just keep picturing Alex. She must have repeated that half a dozen times.

They took their pills, and Ganns remembered feeling a little nauseous, then he woke up on the floor in the facility. In the place Billy called the Titor Center.

Picture Alex, she said. Over and over. Then they were here.

His muscles were starting to relax, and he found he could wiggle his fingers, but the guards had their hands around both his biceps, and they were strong. They were lifting him up when Ganns decided to give it a try. He pictured Darryl. He focused very, very hard on picturing Darryl.

———————

She'd wasted thirty minutes trying to convince Alex that she could recover Ganns faster than they could, then her argument was undermined.

"Look," Alex said, "Ganns is a reasonable man. He's a thoughtful man. He's also a scared man. Catching people on the run isn't your area of expertise, but if we find him, and if he's still scared, you and I will go to him, okay? That's where you can help. But you can't help find him."

Sh'Nae hated to admit it, but Alex's words were completely reasonable. Then again, it seems they always were.

"Besides," she added. "Security has us locked in, and that isn't going to change. They don't fool around with procedures. They follow them to the letter. We'll be on lock down until he's caught, and there's no negotiating that."

There was a tap on the door then, and the same security guard opened the door and stuck his head in. "All clear," he said.

"Did you catch Ganns?"

"Negative. Alicia and Cindy had him and were loading him up, but he shifted."

"Shit," Alex said. She looked at Sh'Nae with a look that Sh'Nae took as concern. As much concern as Alex was probably capable of.

"Excuse me," came another voice. Dr. Looman squeezed past the guard. "I wanted to tell you both, so whichever one of you finds him can let him know."

"Let me guess," Sh'Nae said. "He's got the liver thing, right? NAS?" Looman nodded. "He does."

"Ganns knew you'd tell him that, and he told me so. You're just predictable now."

"Predictable or not, he's got a few short and painful days to live unless we get him back here."

"If we get him back here, from what you said, it doesn't matter in the long run. He won't live anyway, right?"

"That's right."

"Then he won't be back. If you guys were trying to get him to bend your way with this, it didn't work. You did just the opposite. In fact, you're probably why he shifted."

Alex shook her head. "We're not trying anything, Sh'Nae. It's simply the truth."

Sh'Nae nodded. She believed Alex, mostly. Not because she was officious, but because intuition told her to.

"Do you know where he might have gone?" Dr. Looman asked.

"Most likely he's back in New Orleans, but he's lived all over the country and traveled all over the world. He could be anywhere. And anywhen, too. I guess." Sh'Nae thought about it. What would be his top priority if he wasn't here with her? "He'll want to help still. He'd try to find Darryl."

"Is she clear, doctor?" Alex asked. Dr. Looman nodded. "If we can find Ganns with Darryl, our plans haven't changed. Let's keep going."

"Our plans?" Sh'Nae asked.

Alex paused, searching Sh'Nae's face before speaking. "Our plans are to find Darryl. When we find Darryl, I can do what I'm to do, which is stop the presentists from using Darryl to collapse realities. You'll want to do that, because in the process of stopping them, we save Darryl's life. What the presentists want to do is have him shot, as Robert Charles, in the riots. That's when they think he was trapped between the living and the dead, and that's where they think their window is."

"How? What do they do that's different this time?"

Alex shook her head. "We don't know. They've tried this multiple times, and it's always failed. They've never tried it with Darryl though, and they've talked themselves into believing that he's their gamechanger. I don't know if they think just having Darryl there does it, or if they have to do something else as well. We know they think Darryl's trapped between realities, so that must have something to do with it. All that isn't important if we can get to him, though."

"Why is that?"

"We'll get in, make sure that Darryl gets to where he's supposed to be shot, but ensure he makes a different decision. That changes his trajectory, and results in there being no chance in Darryl collapsing realities."

"What about all the other Darryls. Or Roberts, I guess. Why not use one of them?"

"He's the only one who's different, in all realities. He's the only one who shifted when he was killed. The rest were simply killed, one way or another. That's why they want him."

"Why do I think what you said is easier said than done?"

"I have no idea, because it won't be easy. Do you have a better idea? These presentists, they'll stop at nothing to realize their beliefs. They're killers, and besides them we'll be surrounded by angry rioters. No, it won't be easy. Understand that we're not going alone, and we're not planning on subterfuge. We're taking in a well-armed team and, after we know where Darryl is, we don't give a damn who sees us. That gives us an advantage the presentists won't have."

"What about us?"

"We stay down. Our security team will handle the rioters and the presentists."

"If things go amiss?"

"We get out the same way we got in."

"What if we can't get Darryl? Do we still leave?"

"If necessary. I told you that I'm not here to save Darryl. My job is to stop the presentists. We'll save him, though. If we can. It should be the easiest way to undo their plan."

Sh'Nae didn't answer. She just stared as Alex continued. "Look, I've always been straight with you, and I'm being straight now. Have you got a better option?"

Shaking her head, Sh'Nae slumped.

"This is a mission, and we don't take people on missions who haven't got a role to fill, which means you have one. If Ganns was here, he'd have one as well. Your roll is to identify to us which man is Darryl, because we don't know. We've seen Robert Charles, and we know they're supposed to be like brothers, but we don't know what that means. It'll just be two black guys to us. You have to help us there."

Sh'Nae looked up. "Just two black guys?"

Alex paused, waiting for more, but when it didn't come, she continued. "We'll brief here in another thirty minutes, then we go. You'll get there the same way you got here. If you're right, we'll also see and retrieve Ganns."

"There's no need to. You said we can't help him, so let's not pretend." Sh'Nae crossed her arms tightly.

"C'mon, I'll introduce you to the team and its commander."

"I can't travel anymore. I don't have…those things?" She looked down at her clothes. "I don't have anything."

"This is like a military operation, and we pack light. There was a term, back in your day. Shock and awe. That's our approach. We go in all wearing the same jumpers and the same packs. We don't fit in, we frighten. People get out of our way. We get what we want, and we get out."

Sh'Nae nodded, not knowing what to say.

CHAPTER SIX

Year: 1900
Location: New Orleans, Louisiana

He woke up muddled, surrounded by sultry air and raucous sounds. All the noises came from somewhere behind him, but they weren't immediate. The area was shadowed and tight, with one wall inches from his face and wet floor he was stretched across soaking into his pants and shirt. Slowly he sat up and looked around.

The brackish smell he knew immediately—New Orleans. Nothing else looked familiar. He looked toward the noise, and saw a crowd of people milling about in the street at the end of the alley he'd awakened in. They were dressed in linens and coats, and nearly all of them wore hats. In the other direction he saw a hodgepodge of buildings, not aligned at all, and a shadowy figure jogging the opposite direction. He didn't know what to do with either direction.

One thing Ganns did know was that it worked. That thing that Alex explained, it worked. He was a doubter, he'd be the first to admit it, but only so far as the evidence wasn't contrary to his doubt. Here there was evidence. Real evidence. It was possible that he'd been tasered, or whatever, on that island, and just woken up somewhere else. But his nose wasn't lying and this wasn't the same place he'd just been.

Sitting up from the puddle he'd awakened in, Ganns found his pants soaked and filthy. The idea of introducing himself to strangers in a strange land, in a strange time, conflicted with his vision of approachability. He had to fit in somehow, and looking like he'd pissed himself probably wouldn't work. Ganns decided to hide for a bit, if only long enough to dry. Which would work, since he needed to work out, logically, where Darryl would be anyway. New Orleans was a big city.

He wasn't far from the end of the alley and the people making all the noise were clear enough to see. They were singularly men, white men, and about half of them were armed with something capable of violence: some carried firearms, but others carried axes and pitchforks and still others held sticks or ropes. Most were grim, but some were loud and taunting. They were dressed wrongly, because it was hot, and most were wearing long pants and long sleeves. Some were wearing coats.

He pushed back against the wall to the hollow of a shadow and stared at the dirt and pebbles. It smelled like New Orleans, but something wasn't right. Something besides the clothing, but he couldn't figure out what. After waiting a few minutes, until the crowd continued past. What he needed was answers, but he suspected those wouldn't be coming any time soon. Without other options, he stood up and slowly walked in the direction opposite that of the crowd. He could find a restaurant, maybe. Or a store. Somewhere where he could browse and think without worrying about hiding.

After walking a block, he stopped and leaned against a house, stretching out his legs and bending at the waist. That thing, that traveling thing, was hard on a guy.

The alleyway he found himself in wasn't really what he'd call an alleyway. Not in the traditional city sense. I wasn't a poorly maintained and filthy strip of asphalt between two parallel rows of buildings. Instead, it was an irregular space, its floor earthen, and at points it wasn't wide enough for even a small car to get through. There were buildings at the center of the block which didn't face a street on any side, nor did any of them really have a yard. While they were brick and wood and plaster and iron, they were also old and in disrepair.

Ganns paused, looked back at the street, and then forward through the alleyway. Then he hung his head in realization.

He'd not only changed where he was, he'd changed the *when*.

If the logic followed, that he was here because he thought of Darryl and shifted, then Darryl was here. Ganns had no idea about the when, though. New Orleans was an old city, at least by American standards.

It would be easier if he could find Darryl, but how? He couldn't just wander around asking about him. It would help if he knew why Darryl came here, or was brought here, whatever it was.

At the end of the alley he found a cross street, one also made of hardpacked soil. The alley continued forward, and each byway was lined with houses of the same ilk. They were brick or wood, some long and straight while others were long, tall, and straight. Not one was just square. There were more balustrades in immediate sight than he'd seen in his entire life.

One of the other things he noticed was the eyes. There were windows opening to the alleyway and, as he walked, he saw faces peeking out. Dark faces with pale eyes. They looked less like they didn't want to be seen, and more like they really weren't there.

He crossed the next street and continued down the alley, only to find angry white men milling where the next block ended. There was at least a dozen of them, with one yelling madly and the others hupping their consent. Ganns pressed against the wall and waited for them to move on.

The house he stopped at was L-shaped, with a window at the end of the lower leg. He pushed closer to the wall and peered out, watching the men. They weren't moving on at all, but instead were walking around and shouting challenges. Ganns heard them shout coon and jigaboo, whallop and dangle. If it weren't so goddamned frightening, it'd be funny. It was like they didn't know any real words.

He leaned against the wall and closed his eyes. This shifting thing, it took a lot out of him. He imagined he'd get used to it, like staying up late, but he didn't want to. He didn't even want to know that such a thing existed. The one world he was accustomed to had been difficult enough, he didn't need any more. But here they were, and they weren't going away.

He looked around the house toward the street again, and saw that the men were walking, albeit slowly. He guessed they were trying to egg on some of the folks in the houses, trying to get them to come out and fight, but there weren't any takers. Ganns was glad for that, because he didn't think he could just watch someone get lynched, but neither did he think he could do anything about it. Buffoons don't come with reasoning skills, and these buffoons were hardly capable of speech.

Then he heard a scuffing coming from the opposite direction and looked up to find a black man jogging his direction. The man wore the same kind of clothes that the others had. His hair was cut close to his head and his face and neck were dripping with sweat. As he jogged, he lifted both of his hands to show Ganns his palms. Not knowing what to do but suspecting the guy was showing him he meant no harm, Ganns did the same back. He puffed up to the wall and leaned beside Ganns.

"Why we hiding?"

"There's a bunch of angry men the next street over."

"Angry white men? Why are you hiding from angry white men? You're safe."

Ganns nodded. "Until I open my mouth, which I always do."

"Hah. Yeah, I understand. I noticed the clothing. You're not from these parts, are you?"

"Not remotely. Who are you, sir?"

"Name's Wallace. I've seen clothes like that before, back when I was at the Titor Center. Seems like forever ago, but it wasn't."

"You've been to the Titor Center?" Ganns looked around, like he was suddenly expecting more visitors.

"Yeah, went there for training, but I just got back. I'm a local. That's why they recruited me."

"I have no idea who 'they' are." This guy was talking with both ends of his tongue, but Ganns decided the less he himself said, the better. "I'm just here looking for a friend."

The yelling from the street started getting louder again. Ganns looked past the end of the house. When he didn't see anyone, he started searching elsewhere. It sounded like it was coming from the opposite direction, the direction Wallace came from.

"We need to get inside," Wallace said. He tapped on the window, then walked to the opposite end of the house. Ganns followed. The street was clear, so Ganns offered to go knock on the door, but Wallace declined. "They won't let you in, white boy," he said. He went and knocked, then spoke to the homeowner. Wallace was motioning for Ganns to come up when the door opened, and a woman stuck her head out. When she saw Ganns she pulled back in and slammed the door shut.

"He's with me. C'mon, lady." He tapped on the door again, staying as close to it as he could. The front of the house was practically on the property line and just a few feet from the street. There wasn't any cover.

He rapped again. And again. And again. Finally, the door opened a crack and Wallace started talking again, his voice low. After a few words, Wallace motioned Ganns forward and they went in.

With thick curtains drawn over the windows, the inside of the house was a twilight that Ganns had trouble adapting to at first. There was a single lamp burning on a table in the corner, and a shadowy hole at the center of the far wall spoke of the direction to the rest of the house, but that was all he could see. He could hear, though.

"What's your name, boy?" It was a man's voice, deep and calm. Ganns tried to turn to the direction it came from.

"Ganns. Thank you fo…"

"Stop talking." Ganns found he was facing the wrong direction, as the voice was at his side now. "You just stand there." Something hard pressed against Ganns' side, and it felt like a muzzle.

"The only reason you're in here is because he said you're trying to help another black man. For that I'll give you one small chance. That's it. I'd just as soon cut your throat."

Thinking it wise, Ganns showed his empty palms again. As his eyes grew accustomed to the dusky room, he looked around.

It was simple, with a table (the one holding the lamp) and four chairs. The walls were bare and pale, like plaster, and the floor was slatted wood. A pair of boots sat on the floor next to the door, but otherwise, the place was empty. Except for the man and woman standing there beside him, of course.

The woman was dressed in something slight, a simple and shapeless dress from the shoulders to her knees. She wore her hair pulled back tightly into a bun, held with what appeared to be a ribbon. Because of the lighting, everything appeared in black and white.

The man was wearing thick pants, pants which dragged the floor and hardly creased across his bare feet. He wasn't wearing a shirt at all, exposing a thin chest between broad, almost spherical shoulder caps. His neck was slight, and his chin jutted forward. His eyes were huge, as was the revolver he held in his right hand.

"You just sit yourself in a chair over there, yank. I'm fast with this," he bobbled the revolver's tip up and down, "so move slow. Clarissa, can you get us some tea?" The woman nodded and left.

As Ganns was walking toward the table, Wallace told him to sit on the far side, by the wall. Then Wallace asked the man with the gun if they couldn't all go sit. "Spittin' white people aren't our only problem right now, Garrison," he said. "In fact, they might be helpful right now."

Surprisingly, Wallace started out by addressing Ganns instead of Garrison.

"New Orleans is like no city you know, Ganns. Not in my time, and not in your time. It's a city of layers, like wood grain, only no one grain layer touches another. It's a city of gaps. On the surface, we love, but we seethe underneath. Garrison here, I've never met him before, but from his words I knew he'd be an Andryist. I could tell that within three sentences. I, too, am an Andryist."

"I have no idea what that is."

"You heard Garrison. Don't talk." Wallace didn't gesture or raise his voice, but he was past firm. While it made Ganns bristle, he suspected that this Wallace guy wasn't as angry as Garrison obviously was. It looked like manipulation. Besides, Garrison had crossed his

116

arms so he could keep the revolver trained on him. That was disconcerting.

Wallace turned back to Garrison.

"There's a bit afoot today, things you don't know about. Things that if I try to explain, you'll choose to point your hogleg at me instead of him. So many plots, it's dizzying. So many different sides to this story. I haven't a clue. No clue at all."

"You're not giving me a reason to believe you."

"Let's talk about the white people. They're rioting because there's a black man out there right now shooting policemen. He's going to kill a few more. He'll shoot more than twenty people before he's done."

"How do you know what he'll do?"

"I know, okay? I know. I was learned."

There was a pause at the table, a pause struggling to break through the evening heat and stifling animosity, but it failed.

"I know about Robert Charles and the people he shoots. He's a friend of mine and has been since we was kids. He's not with any group, but he pushes Bishop Turner's rag and he's known for it. He's the one who has the white people pissing themselves.

"There's the Andryists, and the streets full of angry white people and a shootin' nigger, that's our dream. Why? Because we get to go out and shoot back."

"But you don't have any iron in your hand, do you?" Garrison asked.

"Not yet, but it's still light outside. Be smart about it, man," Wallace said to him. "We'll get there.

"There's this other group, the one I can't explain, who have a different idea about how history happens. They see how it was, then go back and change it. Anyone else see something wrong with that?"

"Can I talk now?" Ganns asked.

"No," said Garrison, but Wallace nodded. "He can, because I asked the question," he said.

"Because they don't believe they're just changing history. They believe they're creating a new world, a world which has never been before."

"What the hell are you talking about, white boy?"

"Hear him out, Garrison."

"It's hard. They describe the same world, multiple times over, all at once, with each one going in a different direction."

Garrison stared at him for a few seconds, then waved it off.

"If it were true, they wouldn't be the same world, would they?"

"I guess that depends on what makes a world, doesn't it?" Wallace asked.

Clarissa came in then, with two mason jars of tea in one hand and one in the other. She handed the two to Garrison and Wallace and the one to Ganns. "You get no sugar," she said, slamming it down in front of him. Instead of angering, Ganns receded. Anger, right now, wouldn't help him.

"The way they see it, every time there's a shift in events, something big, there's a new world. Don't ask me how this works, because it makes no sense to me. The important part is that this time they want to bring all the timelines together. They want just one world, the thing that most people already believe in, and they want a chance to choose which one we get. They want their world.

"What does that mean to me?" Garrison asked. "I'm already in that world. This is bullshit."

"The world they want might be the world you want. It might not. I don't know. What I do know is that the men trying to change things have a focus I can't believe in."

"What's that?" Ganns asked.

"In their world, there's a black United States, here in the south, and a white United States up north. They're two different countries."

"Sounds like I'd like these men," Garrison said, giving Wallace a small smile.

"Me, too," said Clarissa. "The only thing better would be no white states."

"If they…" Ganns began.

"Shut up!" the other three yelled at him at once. Ganns did.

The table was quiet for a few moments before Clarissa spoke up again. "Do you know how they're doing it? Do you know anything like that?"

"Yeah, I learned a few things." Wallace said. "There's a guy, the guy Ganns here was protecting, who's supposed to be a part of it. He doesn't know much, though. There's the other guy, Robert Charles, who I've known my whole life. He's the one who's out there shooting white folk, and he's a part of it, but he doesn't know it. The people who want this to happen, they're trying to get the two of them together. They think it'll be what's needed. There's a problem with that plan, though."

"What's that?" Garrison asked.

"Me. See, they recruited me to help them. They trained me some, told me the way things are supposed to go. They filled me in on all of their plans. But unlike them, and maybe unlike you, I don't think two different countries is the right answer. I planned on undoing this somehow. Then something came along, something I don't understand, and one of the guys, Darryl, ran off. He's the friend of Ganns here. That bothers me, because it ain't in their plan and it ain't in my plan. We're in a different world than either of us knows, which means something."

"What?" Clarissa asked. "Means what? Means we don't know what the future holds? What's new about that? Without you here at my dinner table, I already didn't know what the future held. Now I know that I don't know. No big-ass deal."

"Clarissa!" Garrison chided.

"You men, always thinking about what could be. I'm too busy thinking about what is."

"Hush, Clarissa."

"Hush yourself, asshole!" She stood and started collecting the glasses, the whole time not taking her eyes off Ganns. "This would all be better, all of it, without this muthafucka here. And you know if I said that, I mean that." She went off toward the kitchen.

"I believe it," Ganns said to himself, knowing that Garrison and Wallace were watching him. They didn't respond.

"Let's say I believe you, and I don't," said Garrison. "This is some weird ass shit. But let's just say that I do, for the sake of conversation. What's next?"

"That's the problem. If you think you know what's going to happen, you can change it. If you don't think you know what's going to happen, then what?" Wallace was talking low, as if he didn't want someone to hear.

"I'll tell you what," Garrison said. "You do what you would do. What the hell did you do before these people came along and trained you? Did you think you knew what was going to happen? Fuck no. But you did shit. You made decisions, even if it was only to get up and go to work. You made those decisions based on what you did know, you did it all, then you learned when you fucked up. Let's just keep doing the do."

Ganns looked from Garrison to Wallace, then nodded. He wanted to open his mouth but thought better of it.

"What do you know? What can we count on?" Garrison added.

"The rest of my team was staging in the streets," said Wallace. "If they've seen the white people already rioting, and they must have, they know it's not going down the way they expect. That won't stop them. This isn't their first time trying, and they're tired of things not working."

"Are they going to know where Darryl is?" Ganns asked. "Can we use them to find him?"

"No, that was my job. I was supposed to deliver Darryl." He paused for a second, then hung his head. "Shit."

"What's up?" Garrison asked.

"They knew they were being undone, by others, and they killed one. Belly's going to automatically think I'm part of that. He'll execute me without thinking twice."

Clarissa walked back in and retook her seat. "We weren't going out unarmed," Garrison said. "You got a pistol for me?"

"Yeah, I have three. We're going to look for your friend. His friend." Garrison pointed at Ganns.

"You have three guns?"

"I do. This one for me," he waved his hog leg, "a similar one for you, and Clarissa carries a snub-nosed revolver everywhere. Which she'll need, because she's going to be watching you." Garrison pointed at Ganns. "There's a lot of sides here, white boy, but no matter which one you're on, I know it's not mine."

"That's a fact," Clarissa said. "I'm on the side for getting some rope." She got up and left the room again.

"Darryl is my friend," Ganns said. "He's the whole damn reason I'm here."

Wallace shrugged. "So you say. I've heard a lot of things in the last couple months, and I have no idea what to believe. With white people out there looking to string niggers up, I'm not trusting you."

"You trusted me when you walked up to me," Ganns said.

"Only because you were on the path Darryl was on and you're wearing those clothes. Because you were white, and you were hiding from the white people. I talked to you because you were different."

"Doesn't it still?"

"Yeah, it does still. You haven't been shot yet. But that doesn't mean I want you walking beside me. We're going to have to stay out of sight, at least until the sun goes down. I'm not sure you would help us with that, so Garrison's right. You're staying here."

Clarissa came back in with a loop of twine and a large kitchen knife. "Ain't rope," she said, "but that don't mean you're lucky."

Garrison stood up and, holding his pistol at the ready, he motioned Wallace over to tie Ganns up. "Just the hands behind his back," Clarissa said. "I may need to move him from here to the back room if he starts hollering, and I ain't big enough to drag the boy."

"What if he runs?" Garrison asked.

"Then I'll shoot his pasty back." She looked toward the back of the house. "I don't want to stay up here where he can be heard too well if the crackers come about. Let's walk back." She looked at Ganns. "I regret it, but you'll be more comfortable back there, too. We has a couch." She stepped back, pulled a small pistol from the folds of her skirt, and aimed it at Ganns. "Tie the boy up," she finished.

Wallace did the tying, trying to find the sweet spot between a rope too loose to hold and a rope too tight to let blood flow. He struggled with it, making and remaking the knots he drew. When he was done, he pulled on Ganns' wrists, trying to separate them. They held.

"We have to git now," Garrison said. "You got this, Clarissa?"

"I got this," she replied.

They did have a couch, and a love seat, and if Ganns had seen either in an antique shop back in California, he'd have snapped them up. Not because they were beautiful, but because they were real. The legs and frame were smooth mahogany, and the border of cloth was pinned to the wood with a series of brass brads which screamed age and sophistication. In this house, it was just furniture, musty-smelling and somewhat faded. He sat down on one end, expecting his guard to take the other side of the couch, but she chose the love seat, which sat on the opposite wall. He squirmed some, trying to get comfortable, but the couch hurt his back. Maybe he wouldn't have bought it.

She didn't say anything, but instead chose to sit there and stare at Ganns. Her gaze was venomous, with her eyes clear and her jaw set, and Ganns knew it had to do with a lot more than just him and just then. Part of him was sorry for her, for all of them, for the crap they had to put up with in the American south. It didn't matter what year this was, did it?

He also suspected that she didn't give a rat's ass about his feeling sorry. She wasn't angry. She was made of anger. Steeped in anger. It flowed from her, and Ganns didn't know what to do with that. There wasn't a way to rationalize with rage. At least, not one he understood.

He squirmed a little.

"Can I lie down?" he asked. But she didn't answer. She didn't move. She was like a statue. Slowly Ganns fell over onto one shoulder. He'd left enough space to the couch arm that he could bend his knees and bring his heels up to his butt. This had to be less threatening. This had to be better for her. But if it was, he couldn't tell. She just stared at him, motionless.

The back twinge was helped by his position, with his neck bent down (they had couches, but no pillows). Still, he wasn't willing to ask for anything. It wouldn't work, and it might make her angrier. If that was possible.

As if she was reading his mind, she said "You thinking I'm a bitch, aren't you? Well, you right." Ganns didn't answer, and she continued. "I'm one angry bitch, I'll tell you what." She stood, then started pacing the room. It was only as wide as the house, maybe twelve or fifteen feet, but it was longer, and she went the long way. This meant she paced into his line of sight, then back out, then back in, but Ganns didn't need to see her. He could hear her bare feet scuffing on the dusty floor. He could feel the ebb and flow of her passion. It was palpable.

On one trip past, she paused before him and squatted, pressing the muzzle of her pistol against his nose and pushing until it slipped off and hit his upper lip. Reflexively Ganns pulled his head back. She didn't say a word and her face remained frozen, her eyes locked on his. Then she stood and started pacing again. It was then that Ganns knew he couldn't wait this out. He also knew he didn't know what he was going to do. Even if she weren't armed, even if his hands were free, he couldn't take her. The woman looked to be carved from coffee-colored stone.

"I was twenty-two," she started. Ganns nodded to himself. Good. She'd talk. "Yes," he started, but she snapped. "Shut up! I'm talking and you listening. You fucking men. You never listen."

Ganns waited.

"I was twenty-two," she repeated. "So, this was a few years ago. Me and Garrison, we were a pretty new thing. Didn't live here yet, because we lived in an upstairs room on Stafford, across the river a ways. I liked it over there, up to that point.

"I was pregnant then, and I spent most of my time in our room watching the world go by. I'd see people walking up and down, wagons going to market up on 1st Street, all kinds of things. Garrison was working on the docks at night, leaving me to tip around quietly during the day and alone at night. Late one night, after I should have been asleep, I was bowed up. I opened the window and went back to bed, to lie on the sheets and sweat some more. There were some street noises still, like conversations, but the day's hullabaloo was gone. But then there came a spitting noise. Angry man noises and some scurrying, and I crossed my dark room to look."

She stopped in front of Ganns, but not because he was there. She was looking at the ceiling now, for a few seconds, then she shook it off and began pacing again.

"There in the street strode a handful of white men, which we do here. We mix it up. But these were yelling white men, and one of 'em had a long gun over his shoulder and another carried a sack. They were spread two by three and cattywampus, and their walk and words told everyone they were looking for trouble. If there'd been folk in the street before, it were cleared now.

"So I watched.

"Here's something I learned later, but I'll tell you now. These men had gone to a woman's house, a black woman's house, for the sole reason of lynching. Six white men gonna lynch a single black woman. She was a sharp cookie and wasn't there when they looked, so they burnt her place up and went out looking for more trouble. Outside our place, they were still looking.

"Opposite me and down a couple houses there was a shadow beside the doorway, and it was clear that it was someone. Someone with nowhere to go. I don't know if he was trying to get in the door or not, but I would have been. When I saw him, he wasn't moving. He was standing completely still, like a spooked doe. I guess one of the white men saw him too, because there was a holler. When the holler hit, the shadow tried to get away, but there wasn't any getting away. He moved like an old man, with his feet hardly leaving the street and his head bent forward.

"The men ran to him, with the one carrying the sack leading the charge. He brought it down on the back of his head, and then the man disappeared. They were standing, they were kneeling, they were kicking and punching and screaming. The only one not playing was the one with the long gun. He was standing aside, watching the street, up and down, with a smile that was all teeth." She stopped telling the story there, but kept pacing, and she was moving quicker now. Her steps were broad, and her arms were swinging until nearly parallel with the floor. Ganns kept waiting for the pistol to fly out of her hand, but she had a good hold on it. He wanted to say something, anything, but between her speed and her warning, he didn't plan on opening his mouth again. Regardless how out of character that was for him.

"As far as fuckin' white people go, this one ended better than most. The man, he lived for a few days. Two, maybe three. Half of the white men paid a price, which is a damn sight better than what usually goes. Three of 'em went to jail for some time. Not a lot, I imagine. The best part is that other white folk came over and strung a fourth one up. The police had him, but the white folks stopped the police, stole their prisoner, and dangled him. It was the one with the rifle, and they hung him by a porch canopy nearby. A whole crowd of white people swingin' a white man. I wish I could have been there."

She turned sharply, in the middle of the room, and knelt in front of Ganns, putting her face inches from his own. He couldn't see the gun, but he heard her set it on the floor, then she poked herself in the forehead.

"That's why," she said. "Others, lots of others, watched. They were far away. I ended up in the cot next to the old man, listening to him trying to breath until he quit, unable to escape because I couldn't walk yet."

Looking at where she poked herself, Ganns saw scar, thin and perhaps an inch long. He knew then that it wasn't the head wound that kept her beside the old man. She said she was pregnant, but there weren't any signs of children in the house. No laughter. No little feet. No toys. He couldn't help himself now.

"You tried to help," he said.

"Yeah. I tried." Then she picked the gun back up.

———————

Garrison's legs were thinner, but longer, and Wallace was having a tough time keeping up with him. What was really perturbing was that, when they left the house, Wallace thought it was his job to lead the way. As it turned out, this trip was on Garrison.

"You're part of this? All the people coming into town, all the people from all over? Trains and wagons and everything?"

"More than that. More than you know," Wallace said, breathlessly. "Slow it down, Garrison. I can't keep up with you and I don't know what the hell we're doing."

"We're moving because the crackers are lookin' to frog gig us. Two minutes away, then we'll slow it down. Until then, commence to scurryin'." Which Wallace did. After they turned onto Rampart Street and turned directly into a shadowed house short of its intersection with Erato Street, Wallace had a pretty good idea why.

Outside the house it looked abandoned, with the weeds knee-tall and not a single glimmer of light. They strode up to the porch and Garrison broke free with a patterned knock. With a couple clicks, the door opened and they slipped inside.

The room was crowded with shadows and sweat, and there was no way for Wallace to tell how many people were crowded inside. They stood in clusters, spoke in hushed tones, and leaned against their rifles. Wallace and Garrison were checked at the door, but once inside no one paid them any mind. Wallace was amazed at how relaxed everyone seemed to be.

Garrison wove them through the crowd to a back hallway and the room beyond. There was a tall fellow standing in the center of the hallway, his arms dangling at his sides. They were five feet short of reaching the roadblock when Garrison stopped.

"Tell Caspar that Garrison bring news. Tell him it may affect his plans." The roadblock didn't move for a few seconds, as if he was processing the words slowly, but then he turned and went into the back room. A few seconds later he looked back into the hallway and waved them forward. Garrison led the way, with Wallace following slowly, hands in pockets. He didn't trust what was happening.

Half a dozen more people were in the back room, leaving it nearly empty in comparison to the front of the house. Standing at the back was a short man, probably five feet tall, but broad across the shoulders with thick limbs. He was built like a tree stump. The tree stump walked over and looked at both men entering. "Which one is Garrison?" Garrison raised one of his hands but didn't say anything. "What's the news?" Caspar asked.

"He's got to tell it, because it makes no sense to me." Garrison pointed at Wallace. "Tell him, Wallace."

Wallace explained the multiverse and how there were separate groups manipulating the riots and all that was happening around them to get the world they wanted. Caspar didn't move, and he didn't ask questions. He stood completely still and listened. When Wallace finished, the short man scratched at his chin for a second, then nodded.

"So which world we get if we stomp the rioters around the Saratoga house?"

"I don't know. Depends on whether the right Robert Charles gets shot and it depends on whether or not he dies. I think. I'm no expert."

"If another Robert Charles gets shot and killed, not the Darryl one, what happens?"

"Our revolution fails, and we get a mixed America. The multiverse remains a multiverse."

"That same one gets shot and not killed, then what?"

"I think our revolution succeeds, but I don't know for sure.
The multiverse remains a multiverse."

"Your guy gets shot and killed?"

"The multiverse collapses, we get a mixed America and we share it with everyone who has ever been because the dead come back."

"It'll get crowded. Your guy gets shot and not killed?"

"The multiverse collapses into one, our revolution succeeds, and there's no dead."

Caspar nodded. "What if all the Robert Charles' get shot? What if none of them do?" Wallace didn't answer for a few seconds, then he finally said "I have no idea."

"The world is full of dumb fucks, and I'm pretty sure y'all are two of them. That said, let's pretend this is all true. Do I care? No. I live in one world. This one. It barely matters, so others don't matter at all." He walked back to his corner, stood for a few seconds, then walked back.

127

"We can make damn sure Robert Charles gets shot, but I don't think so. The man is on our side. We might prevent him from getting shot. We have enough folks to round up the white people at Saratoga. If any of the Robert Charles get shot, we can't do shit about them dying or not. That leaves us not knowing what's going to happen, right?"

"Pretty much," Garrison said.

"Then nothing changes. We roust up when the big guns in the harbor start shooting and we're going hunting. Tonight, the world changes or tonight we die. One or the other."

Garrison nodded and started to turn away, but Caspar reached out his arm and touched him on the shoulder. "Where you going, brother?"

"I'm done," Garrison said. "I just wanted you to know. I'm heading home now."

"No, no you're not. Once you're in, you're in for good. You two will wait here with us and you'll fight with us. We're going to hell together, friend."

"I need to leave," Garrison said. "My wife needs me."

"We all have wives and children. Let's give them something to live for. And you," Caspar pointed at Wallace, "We need you as well."

"What about my wife? And my friend Robert?" Wallace asked, knowing what answer he'd get.

"Everyone in here is someone's friend," Caspar said. "We're all doing this for each other, and we're all doing it for Robert. You're with him in spirit." Wallace nodded, knowing it was time to take a chance. He just wished he could kiss Countess one more time.

Pulling out his pistol, Wallace quickly stepped to the side of Caspar and put the muzzle up against the man's temple. "I'm leaving," he said quietly.

"You won't get far out there," Caspar replied. "You're threatening to waste lead. Save that for the white man."

"I said I'm leaving," Wallace repeated. "Garrison, you can leave or you can stay. It's up to you."

For once Darryl was thankful for his time on the street. He'd made it as far as the river moving between houses, avoiding the gangs and the people behind doors who tried to usher him in. Avoiding everyone except the dead.

It was a bit of a walk, maybe a mile, and he wasn't sure where he was heading while heading there. It was just a direction, and any direction felt better than none. As he moved on, the rioters thinned out, with the groups being smaller and less boisterous. Watching them move from a distance was like playing with dominoes, because as they moved through the streets windows and doors were slammed. Darryl could imagine the people inside bar ring things down and standing away from the fronts of their houses. If he was in a house, that's what he'd do. But he wasn't. He was on the street, and to be honest that's where he belonged. This felt right. That, in of itself was weird. He wasn't really used to feeling right. But for the first time in his memory, however short that was, this was correct.

While avoiding the rioters wasn't difficult and ignoring the viewers who saw him and tried to save him was downright easy, he was glad he didn't have to avoid the dead. Because they were everywhere, moving about smartly like they were back at the first house Darryl had been in. These dead were in the streets, like the rioters, but some also moved with a purpose. There were several greeting each other, and another time he saw one knocking on a door. They had places to be, these dead. At least most did. Others sat on the street or on porches. Some on tree limbs. It was like a summer shower of dead just ended.

It occurred to Darryl, as he walked, that a few of them waved at him. That made him different than the other living people, but he was used to that. He'd always been different. But they were talking to him and waving at him, like he was popular. Like he was someone. But he wasn't. Was he?

When the houses abruptly ended, leaving Darryl just a stretch of road and swathe of grass away from the Mississippi River, it occurred to him that he was no longer in hiding, and he'd not been hiding for a few blocks. He couldn't remember seeing any living people during that span, because there were just the happy dead.

He continued to a point near the water's edge, where he found a table of thick, wooden planks and four matching chairs. There was another set probably 25 yards to the east, and yet another 25 to the west. If it was a park, it wasn't much of one, but the view was nice. There were ships on the water, a couple iron hulls and a stern wheeler pushing barges of coal. There were a few smaller boats working the water as well, with folks throwing lines and walking back and forth with intent. He expected to see just a few fishermen on the shore, but there weren't any. In fact, he only saw one person, and that one was dead. He was sitting at the nearby table, and when he saw Darryl he motioned him over by patting the arm on the chair beside his own.

"Sit, Robert." The man said, showing a wide grin. Darryl looked around but didn't see anyone else but himself. The man patted the arm again. Darryl went over.

Like many, this guy wasn't dead by obvious means, but he was obviously dead. His eyes were sunken and the bags below them were huge. His brown skin hung loose, like an adult's dress jacket worn by a child. He didn't have any teeth and an array of wrinkles leaked from the outer edges of each eye. There wasn't anything frightening about him, but the dead had long since not frightened him. In fact, he couldn't remember if they'd ever had.

"I saw you coming down the street there and I thought I should send you back. You're going to miss our chance," the dead man said.

"Our chance?" Darryl asked, taking the seat offered. He was starting to think that this was what was supposed to happen. That he'd break away and find a direction unlike that offered by all the people he'd met since running from Sh'Nae. They all seemed to want something from him. "And why'd you call me Robert?"

"Because that's your name. You're Robert Charles."

"My name is Darryl Green."

"Is that what they told you?" The man erupted in a laughter like rolling echoes. "I guess you don't remember, then."

Darryl stared at the man, waiting for him to say something that made sense. Something that Darryl could work with. So far, there'd been nothing.

"We called you our runaway, you know. All the black folk. The white folk didn't have a nickname for you, but they've put their hopes in you, nonetheless. White hope. Who'd have thought?"

Darryl looked around, watching the dead mill, cavort, spread out, and otherwise fill the streets. If there were still marauding white people, they were hidden now. "What about the others?" he asked.

"Others?"

"There are others. Not black. Not white."

"They're here, too. All colors."

Darryl nodded and looked around. Where the river met the shore it made a low, wet sound, like it was licking the earth. He could hear the stern wheeler splashing, its wheel working furiously considering its crawl north. Mechanical noises came from elsewhere, perhaps from the other ships, perhaps from one of the buildings on the dock across the water. But probably not. The water was too wide.

He scratched at the wood. What made this all even odder was that his head was clearer, his thoughts more linear, than he could ever remember. None of the whispy confusion he'd known for years, for every year he could remember. Yet he was surrounded by the wrongest of things. The world was filling up with the dead. Overflowing with the dead.

"Let's get you home, Robert."

"I'm Darryl," Darryl said. "And no. I'm done going where people send me."

"Where you going on your own, then? You can't walk from fate." The man put one hand across Darryl's closest forearm. "You're one of us, Robert. One of them, but also one of us. You can't walk away."

"Why?" Darryl asked. "Why can't you explain this to me? What can't *anyone*? Explain it so I can understand? I just keep going from place to place, doing what people tell me to do. I want to be done!"

The man nodded his head, turning toward the water. In the sunlight Darryl saw that his lips were dark purple, and his teeth were stained with blood. "I got you. You and me, let's take a walk." He got up and took a few steps back toward the houses, then stopped and crossed his arms. "Coming?"

"I don't know."

"You said you wanted to understand."

"I do." Darryl sighed and stood up. "I do."

"Let's go. I'm going to tell you a story."

———————————

"My grandmother wouldn't say the words dead or death, but she'd use other words. People were *departed* or *passed* or *expired*, but no one was dead. Another one of her favorites was to say that folk had gone beyond the veil. That one never made any sense to me, because I didn't know what a veil was until after she was buried. When I did, it still didn't make any sense. The dead don't get married. It didn't make sense until I died.

"Before I get there, you know what's funny about death? The way it's looked at by the living. I remember thinking that when I died that I wanted to go fast, like get hit by a train or something.

"The reason I wanted that is because I didn't want to suffer, and there's some wisdom there. The idea that suffering ends when you pass is laughable. Death isn't a mirror image of life. There's things going on over here that don't go on over there. But at that point where you go, it's pretty close to a mirror image. If your suffering peaks when your heart quits, it's peaking when you sit up on the other side. The pain starts ebbing, but it's still there, because that's the way the veil works. It's just an thin shade of separation.

"Watch the rut there. Don't trip. And let's take 9th Street. It'll be easier.

"Picture that. You're standing in your grandma's bedroom, after she passes on, and you're looking in her mirror. The same mirror she used to scrub and tie her hair in, if she did that kind of thing. Now you're looking in it because she's gone, and you're thinking about her. That's what I did when my grandmother passed. She had a big mirror on the wall, one with a thick, wooden frame. It hung over a tiny desk, and that desk was close to her tiny little bed. She didn't have much, but she had that mirror, and now it was mine.

"Now what the hell was I gonna do with a big-assed mirror? I got my head shaved when my hair got thicker than a fingernail, then let it grow, then got it shaved again. I didn't need a mirror for that. I kept it, though. You know why?"

Darryl walked, staring at his own feet as he went. He shook his head.

"I kept it because my grandmother used to stare into it, it was the only thing she had, and I wanted to be close to her. She was a wonderful woman, my grandmother. She raised me right.

"I think the comfort came from the idea that my grandmother was in the mirror. That she could stare back at me. That she could smile or wave or whatever she wanted. I sometimes imagined her there, not trapped or anything, but just walking up and looking through it at me. She couldn't, of course. She was beyond the veil.

"You ever get told not to start learning? It's good advice. For example, I learned there was more to my grandmother's saying about veils than I ever imagined.

"You said you don't remember anything, right? I mean, if you did, you'd already know everything I'm about to tell you. But if you don't know, I'll let you in on it. Because you'll know it again soon enough. Everyone gets to know the other side.

"To be clear, by the other side I'm not talking of heaven or hell. I wasn't a religious man, because my grandmother wasn't a religious woman. She never did understand why black folk took up with the white man's gods. But then my grandmother was a slave. Not one born into slavery, like I was, but one who came to this damn place in leaky ship smelling of rot and sweat and fear. She almost died, tied up down there. She thinks they all almost died, and she said time enough that they would have been better off if they had. I wouldn't have been, obviously, but I get it. That lash still stings.

"Where was I?

"Yeah. Could my grandmother see through that mirror? Could she see me? No, not then. If I were alive today, she could. You're the reason for that. You're the reason for all these folks being here. You're THE REASON.

133

"You wanted to know this? I'll tell you. It's a miserable thing, dying. The other side may be miserable too, depending on how you're built. It wasn't so for me, but I imagine the socialites want to die again every day. Death is lonely. When you pass to the other side of the veil, you're in the same place you were when you died. You're wearing whatever you're wearing when you died, or at least I was. From looking around, I'd guess that's just the case. The world is all there, just like you left it, but it's only you. There's no one else. Folks talk about getting to heaven or wherever and seeing their ma or their pa, but there's no one. It's just you, I'm tellin' you.

"Though the world looks the same, it's not. There's no weather. I died in the middle of the day, I remember lying in the dirt staring up at the sun, and that's what I saw on the other side. The sun. There wasn't any heat, though. There weren't any breezes. No cicada chirps or gulls laughing. There's just a quiet, unchanging world that's a shadow of the one you left behind.

"It's not all bad. I've never been hungry or thirsty, which is good because there's no food. The river's there, but I can't drink from it because I can't touch it. I dip my face into its surface, and I'm dry.

"Death brings an eternity of a moment.

"If you're thinking about this, and I hope you are, you'll be asking yourself about them over there. That boy, the one that damn near looks like a skeleton and skin, he's hanging on a tree branch. Look at him kick and laugh! Can't do that on the other side of the veil because, though you'd see the tree, you'd never be able to touch it. Why can he do that? It's because of you, Robert.

"Here's the part where we talk about you. I don't know why you doesn't remember. Maybe it's because you straddle the veil?

"The story goes that you lost your cool and started picking off white people, which is funny. I mean, who hasn't wanted to do that? That part alone made you a hero. This next part that I'm about to tell you, don't ask me to explain it. I can't. I know nothing about it, other than folks say that's why we're all here. That's why things are changing.

"What they said was that the white folks surrounded you and shot back. They say that you were standing in front of a window, up on the second floor of some house over on Saratoga, and that you were hit in the chest, that you fell back. When they went up there, all the white folk, they couldn't find you. There was some other poor black fella there, one hiding beneath the bed, and I bet they gave him hell, but there wasn't anyone shot. There wasn't any blood. There was nothing the white folk needed.

"That's when it all started, it's said. That's when the veil began to slide down. The first time I knew something changed I was lying in the road, about where I was when I died. There's nowhere to go and nothing to do when you're on the other side.

"I found comfort where I could. Kind of like with the mirror, I was looking into myself by putting myself where I was when I died. I could think there. It was calming. Then, I felt the rain.

"Rain. Rain, which is water. I opened my eyes to find a thundercloud overhead. Just one. It wasn't a proper storm, but it was dropping a few drops my way, saying "hi" to me. I sat up and saw, down the road, and I saw a wagon traveling the opposite way. I went over and stuck my hand in the Mississippi, and it was cool and wet. It was wonderful, and I thought I was alive again. I thought I was back!

"That joy died its own death shortly.

"First off, there weren't any other people. Or animals, for that matter. None. I could see things, like wagons, moving through the streets. The sun started rising and sinking again, and I saw things float by, like a piece of furniture unloaded into a storefront. It looked like it floated off. What began as joy faded to dread, and suddenly I found myself wondering if I was caught in some haunted place. Me, a dead man, being haunted. Ain't that rich?

"I couldn't take it, so I took my spot in the road again. I closed my eyes, and went back to doing what I did, which was mostly walking through my memories, replaying them over. Sometimes changing them.

"I was a slave for the family owning a hotel, a place we called the Exchange. Inside there was this big room with a round ceiling, kinda like the inside of a ball, that was both grand and miserable. Like I said, I was born a slave, right there. The exchange was all I ever knew. Inside that grand room I watched white men sell my brothers and sisters. Most were sullen and quiet, their eyes down, but some cried and others howled. It was a sight, always. I never got used to that part of things.

"I'd go through those days, lying on the street, thinking my way through letting those people go. Sometimes the chains would all just disappear, we'd rise up and kill the white men. Other times, the white men disappeared with the chains and we would live in the grand room and stare at its beautiful ceiling. I replayed the way I died more than anything. It was a bucking horse, one I was calming, but it weren't taking it. It showed me with a good wallop from both rear legs. I landed on my heard in the middle of the street, stone dead.

"Dreaming about change kept me from looking around, so I didn't have to see the ghosts that creeped me. Every now and then I'd look up, just to see if they were still there, and they were. Sometimes I'd get brave and walk around, but I always saw new ghosts and new things and I didn't like it, which meant I always ended up lying back in the road. I only remember a cart running over me once, and that was funny. It didn't hurt, but I bet it surprised the ghosts when that cart rode up.

"I was lying there, listening to the wind, because I had wind again, and I heard a voice. Let me tell you, that was something! I shot up from the road and started searching around, looking for the source, and after a bit I found it. There was this white fellow, a short guy with a mop of gray hair on his head and another across his chest. His pants were almost shiny, like glass, and he wasn't wearing a shirt or shoes. I figured if he were dead he'd lived pretty well, because he looked plump and happy to me.

"This guy, he calls himself Andre, he grabs my hand and he's shaking it up and down like it's a water pump. He's talking faster than I can hear, and I just kept staring at him. That's when he slows down and says that things are changing. I nodded, because yes, they were. I hadn't seen another man in a lifetime, so they were changing. He tells me that I'll be seeing more than him. He came here looking for whoever was here, and now that he found me and he told me, he was going to go looking for others elsewhere.

"I'm normally not one lookin' for white people to hang around, but it was nice hearing a voice. It was nice shaking a hand. But he said he couldn't stay. He had to keep moving, keep telling people. Then I asked him what he's telling.

"He says that we're going back to the real world, the one we all left. All of us. All of those who died. I stared for a second, then asked him if he was drunk. He shook his head and laughed. Then I asked him if he meant we'd be alive again, and he got quiet pretty quick. "I don't know," he says to me *I don't know how this works. I just know that there's a man who's bring us all together. All the worlds and all the people, all at once. We'll be with the living and they with us. We'll get to see our families and friends.* and he just got all excited again. I asked him how he knew all this, and he says the reason we're alone is because this is our world. I'm in mine. He's in his. Everyone who's ever died is in their own. I nodded, thinking that explained the road and the sun, but it didn't explain the wagon rolling over me. I told him about that, and that's where he says that he knew about all the worlds when he was alive, and he traveled between them. When he was in his world, after he died, and someone came and told him, like he was telling me, that we were going to be free, he decided to visit other worlds and spread the word. Somewhere in there he learned about you, Robert Charles. How you were the one bringing all the worlds together. That's what this is, that's why all these people are here. You've done it, or at least you're doing it.

"Do you understand now, Robert? Do you see what you are to me? To all of us beyond the veil?

"You have to finish what you've started."

———————

As they walked through the streets Darryl felt the occasional pat on his back and saw the smiles and nods. He didn't know if the man was telling the truth, but he knew the rest thought so. It was clear that he was some sort of hero, but he didn't know how, just like he didn't know really if he was Darryl Green or Robert Charles. There wasn't much in his memory before the streets and Sh'Nae.

Was he Robert Charles? He could be. But merging worlds? Was he supposed to merge worlds? Darryl couldn't fathom how'd he'd know about such a thing, much less do it. If what he was told was true, if everyone who died went to their own world, and he was now surrounded by hundreds, maybe thousands of dead people, then it could be true. If there were thousands of worlds here in this one section of New Orleans, how many were in Louisiana? How many in the United States? How many in the world? How many dead people have there ever been?

He couldn't think about it anymore.

"Do you know where I'm supposed to be, then?" he finally asked.

"Maybe," the man said.

"How do you know?"

"It's the place where you got shot, right? The same place. It must be. I suspect it's supposed to happen again. We're going to a house on Saratoga to find out."

"Then what?"

"I have no idea."

The dead were crushing the streets now, rubbing shoulders because they didn't have a choice. This was slowing down their progress, but Darryl wasn't particularly in a hurry. He was still going where people told him to go and still doing what people told him to do. It hadn't ever been a problem before. He hadn't even thought of it before. But it was a problem now. He watched the crowd clear a path as they walked, and he wished they wouldn't.

That was when he heard shouting in voices of a different timbre. They were removed and hollow, but they were also angry. Suddenly realizing he was on the street, right in the middle, Darryl searched around to find the intermittent aspect of three white men coming his way. The dead weren't parting for the white people, because they didn't need to, and the white people were walking through the dead. Darryl instantly knew he had to run, because they wouldn't be ghosts to him, but the dead didn't know. They were oblivious.

Darryl broke off, trying to run back toward the water. He wasn't sure why that was safer, but there hadn't been any marauding white people down there before. He only made it a few steps before he was held up by hands grabbing him from all sides. Hands from all around. The dead were pressing up on him, shaking their heads and denying him his exit. He squirmed and fought, but they wouldn't let go. One foot up and out, an arm on that same side outstretched, trying to find his way free of the hands holding him seemingly everywhere. He kept looking back at the white men, looking forward, looking back, and that's when he saw one white man hand his pistol to another and charge Darryl.

The attacker wasn't a big guy, but since Darryl couldn't roll with the hit it knocked the breath out of him. He struggled against the hands, which held him from his knees to his neck. They pulled and pushed, forcing him into a jerky dance. When the white guy got up off the ground, he pummeled Darryl's ribcage with a series of punches, then tried wrapping his arms around him and twisting him to the ground. Darryl continued his spasmodic response, the pain pulling and pushing his body like a flower in a windstorm. The other two white guys stared at Darryl and his attacker, their faces squinched in confusion. Finally, one started waving his pistol and yelled at his friend to step away from Darryl.

Sh'Nae stood there, her mouth open, watching two of three men beating on Darryl, and Darryl just standing there, his body re bounding from the blows but otherwise held erect. His legs kicked out and back, sometimes simultaneously, leaving him floating in the air. But he didn't fall. Alex wasn't doing anything about it, and Sh'Nae was about to run at the men from the side of the street when Alex held out one hand to hold her back. "Gil," she said quietly, and pointed at the one raising his pistol. Gil's weapon was already shouldered, as were all the security, so it only took him the duration of a nod to take the pistol wielder out.

The other two turned to see where the fire came from, then stepped back from Darryl while the security team advanced on them. A second later, they broke in the direction of the Mississippi.

Though his face was shiny and his clothes undoubtedly hid bruises, Darryl didn't look any the worse for the wear. He didn't even look like he knew they were there or that he'd been saved. Sh'Nae knew the look he was wearing, and she knew it meant he'd descended into a fugue. She started to explain this to Alex, who knew nothing of his states, and quit when she saw both of Darryl's feet floating up off the ground.

He levitated slowly and roughly, not at all like Sh'Nae had seen in the movies. It looked like he was on rough seas, his body bouncing and jostling. As he moved from vertical to horizontal, his body started to move forward.

"Let's follow," Alex said.

"Follow? Let's take him away! Let's get him and go!" Sh'Nae was walking quickly, trying to keep up with Alex. She moved quickly for someone with short legs.

"You see the way he wasn't falling when he was being beat? That wasn't him, that's something else, something that has a hold of him. Trying to pull him away may hurt him."

"Something?"

"The dead, I'm guessing."

"Christ." Sh'Nae didn't say anything more because Alex was right.

"I know. I'm not sure what to do with it, either." Alex, Sh'Nae, and the armed entourage fell in behind Darryl as he started floating down the street, his back about three feet off the ground. He rocked slightly as they went, and his arms were crossed on his chest. His eyes were closed. "Why?" Alex asked herself. "Why, why, why?"

They'd gone only a block when she shook her head as if she was shaking off gnats. "Really?" she asked herself, then added "We're following him, probably to the Saratoga house. Which means it'll be surrounded. Gil, break off and take Sh'Nae around the north and come out on top. Keep her out of sight and keep her protected."

"Bullshit," Sh'Nae said. "I'm staying with Darryl."

"No, you aren't. You're a black woman and we're walking into a race riot of white people. Your being here guarantees an attack. They may attack Darryl, but since he's floating, and they still believe in devils and demons here, maybe they won't. We can't protect you if they all turn our way. Gil?"

One of the security detail on the lefthand side peeled off and stood aside while Sh'Nae caught up with him. "We'll still get there," he said. "We're just not going to walk into the crowd."

"How do you know there's a crowd," Sh'Nae asked. "We haven't got there yet, and everything is changing."

"We don't. There were crowds before, and we work off the best information we have. Come on." He turned halfway, but still waited. Sh'Nae, frustrated and slightly disgusted with herself, broke off and followed him. They only went about ten feet before she turned and watched Darryl, Alex, and the others in the security detail continue slowly down the street. They could only go as fast as Darryl floated, and that wasn't quick. Alex had reorganized them into a straddling shield for Darryl, with herself and two on one side and three on the other. She had a weapon out now, something like a pistol, but with the same odd barrel bulges on it that the rifles had.

"We're not even twenty minutes from the house, and if you and I hurry we can be hiding nearby when they get there." He had one leg forward as if ready to start running, and he was smiling. Sh'Nae didn't want to go and she didn't want to lose sight of Darryl, but Alex's point was valid. She couldn't help him if she were dead. "Yeah," she finally said. "You lead."

They moved left one street from the one they'd been on, then headed forward. He wasn't running, but he was moving in quick spurts and keeping his rifle at the ready. The houses, close as they were, made for good cover with their overhanging porches and huddled trees and bushes. They moved from block to block in a quick fit, the efforts sped up by the space separating them from the yelling and occasional gun blasts somewhere off to their right. This continued for the better part of a mile. "Do you know where we're going?" Sh'Nae finally asked.

"Following this," he said, waving his left arm up in the air. In the fading light she saw that he had something like a watch on, but on its face there was a picture and a blinking red light. She couldn't see the details, but she assumed it was a map. "It gives me the layout and tells me where Dr. Donna is compared to where we are." He kept going as he talked, slowing at the next cross street for a look before moving forward.

"Dr. Donna?" Sh'Nae asked.

"Yeah, but not like a give you a stitch doctor. Something else. Wait a sec." He held an open palm back for a second and went forward to the next cross street. The noises were louder and angrier here, but still had to be at least a couple blocks over. He walked back, facing her. He was a handsome fellow, about as tall as Sh'Nae with a shock of red hair on top. He wore his smile both on his lips and in his eyes. "It's safe, but we should move across the street singularly, and quickly. I'll go first and provide cover for you, okay?" They walked up until he motioned for them to stop, then he moved across at a jog. On the other side, he readied his rifle to his own left, then nodded for her to follow him. She jogged across quickly herself.

"You still got it," he said as she closed. Sh'Nae didn't respond, but the words stuck in her head. Still got what?

They continued up another four blocks, then he motioned for them to turn right.

They went down another two blocks, then paused beneath a live oak pressed up against a home with mud for a porch. Its branches reached out into the street, offering shadows. At the tree's trunk, he squatted. "How far do we have to go?" Sh'Nae asked. He looked at his wrist and shrugged. "Almost twenty blocks that way," he said, pointing down the street they were now on. "Rioters are scattered about, but where we're heading should be the epicenter of it all. We'll have to slow as we get closer." Sh'Nae started walking, but Gil remained seated.

"Wait up. No need getting there before Darryl does, and he's moving slower than we are." He motioned for Sh'Nae to return, but she didn't. She just stood, arms dangling. From her perspective, if she wasn't moving forward, she wasn't doing anything. She had to do something.

"You still don't remember?" he asked.

"Remember what?"

Gil unzipped a large pocket in the middle of his right thigh and pulled out a black tube about three inches long and an inch in diameter. He popped off the plastic lid and pulled out something which immediately unfolded into a thin and flat sheet. After pressing a corner of it, the surface lit up. He flicked at it a few times, then held it up to Sh'Nae.

She took it and found a picture on the screen. There were three people in the picture: Alex, Ganns, and herself. They were all giving a thumbs-up and smiling at the camera. Sh'Nae caught her breath. There'd never been a picture like this taken anywhere. There couldn't have been.

"I don't believe it," she said, handing the square back to Gil. "That's some kind of photo trick."

"No trick, Sh'Nae. I took the picture at the end of our training. I was there. Our whole team was there."

Sh'Nae looked down the street toward where Darryl was heading. "Was Darryl part of this team?" she asked.

"No, but the mission was built around him. Also, his name isn't Darryl. It's Robert Charles."

All the doubts Sh'Nae shielded off Ganns came rushing in like a wave. Not just doubts with Alex, but all of them. His doubts about the federal government. His doubts about his hometown of Hollywood. His doubts about everything that ever happened somewhere outside of his immediate line of sight. Everything. While the picture wasn't credible to her, neither was traveling across the multiverse or watching her friend carried by the invisible dead. This picture itself was hardly the weirdest of it all, but in aggregate it was almost too much to take. She looked down at Gil looking up and her, feeling it all at once. She felt a twitch.

"You brought me here on purpose? Out of the way? If you were really in security, you'd know how to keep a secret. But you didn't. Who are you? Why else would you tell me that I'm part of this if you didn't want to change what I'm to do afterward?" The twitch grew, first in her abdomen, then down her right leg. She was ready to bolt, but she knew he could stop her with his rifle, if that was his mission. She didn't know if she had anything to do with Alex's plans. It might be she was meant to die here.

"Look, it's not that."

"I don't want to hear it. I'm going to keep moving." She turned and headed down the street.

Ganns kept his eyes closed, because for some reason that helped with the pain. His back felt tweaked when he was on the couch, but when she grabbed him by his collar and yanked him to the floor, it ruptured into pain that spread across his abdomen from behind his stomach to mid-chest. She yanked him hard, but not that hard. It felt like he'd been shot.

Keeping his eyes closed also meant he didn't have to see her face, which was screwed tight with anger. When he did take a quick glance, he saw that she looked like a skull caricature. Eyes pulled up tight and teeth clenched, she was pacing the room and shifting the pistol back and forth between her two hands. Once she'd set the pistol on the table and disappeared, coming back with a long knife to pace with, and twice now she'd traded back and forth between them, like she was trying to give equal mileage to both.

Ganns kept thinking about shifting out of there, out of the house and on to somewhere different, but he didn't know where he'd land. He expected to find Darryl when he came to New Orleans, because that was who he was thinking about. But he didn't see Darryl. He hadn't seen Darryl. He couldn't go back to the Titor Center because they'd have him locked up in a flash. He suspected that Sh'Nae wouldn't stay there anyway, because she'd be coming here to find Darryl. He had to remain, hopefully without dying at this madwoman's hands.

He'd tried to keep her talking, but she'd quit using sentences completely. Sometimes she screamed at him and other times she let loose with curses, and it was clear where her mind was. He was ready to shift, when he had to, he just didn't want to until it was necessary.

It was all wrong, every bit of it, but Ganns didn't know what right looked like anymore. He didn't deserve to die here after trying to help Darryl. She didn't deserve to lose her child. Sh'Nae didn't deserve to worry and search, and Darryl didn't deserve the ghosts that haunted him. Everything was upside down. The world was made of inequity, he knew that, but he felt there'd been something he could do about it before. All his art was about exposing these things. Now, he was the one exposed.

She was standing before the front door, staring at it as if it might open. She had the pistol in her hand again, and the hand it was in was half raised, as if she intended to shoot at whoever came through the door. Ganns listened and heard voices. The muffled voices of men. They were probably out on the street. He couldn't hear anything else until Clarissa started to whisper.

"Come on," she said. "C'mon, c'mon, c'mon." She repeated the mantra over and over, her eyes locked on some point past the door. She backed up a couple steps, then stepped forward again.

She's losing it, Ganns thought. I must be ready. The voices faded away and he closed his eyes again, listening for her pacing to restart. She was moving around, and she was close, but he didn't want to look. He didn't want to see. Until she touched the tip of his nose, at which point Ganns opened his eyes.

She was sitting cross-legged in front of him, and both the weapons were on the floor to her right. Which meant both her hands were empty, and that gave him some small amount of relief. She was gently pushing against the tip of his nose with one finger and staring into his face, and it felt like it lasted forever. Finally, she pulled her hand away and dropped both into her lap. Her back was bent, and her face was awash with grief now instead of anger.

"Do you know what you are to me?"

He knew to keep his mouth shut, he knew that was the right thing to do. But he wasn't capable, and that was the story of his life.

"I'm every white man?" he asked. She nodded. "Yeah, you are. Every white devil ever."

"I'm sorry, Clarissa. I'm sorry for all of them. They were wrong. They are wrong."

"Wrong and right don't matter though, does it?" she asked. "If it mattered, taking things wrong and making them right would make the pain go away. That white man swinging, that would have made the pain go away, but it didn't. Nothing makes the pain go away."

Ganns nodded, sending sheets of pain up his back into the base of his neck. His chest was heavy.

"I don't know if I've ever known right, to be honest. Don't know if I'd recognize it. Do you know right, white devil?"

Ganns tried to nod, but he couldn't. Finally, he said "yes", just one simple "yes."

"What's it look like?"

He had poetry in his mind. It looks like a child's smile. Like water when you thirst. He didn't think it wise. Not now. "It doesn't look like this," he said, finally. "It doesn't look like here."

"That's no lie," she said, still staring him in the face. "You okay, white boy? You're looking kinda blue."

"I hurt. I need to stretch." He tried to breath. "Can you cut me loose? I won't go anywhere."

"Not much chance of that happening, so yeah, you won't go anywhere. Just lie there and look bad, then. Look blue." She picked up her gun and set it in her lap, staring over Ganns at the back of the couch. "Look blue," she repeated, then she grabbed the gun and stood quickly. "I need to get out of here. I need to find Garrison and get the hell out of here. I need to find what right looks like." She paced across the room again. "You hear me, devil? I need right!" She went to the door, cracked it, and looked out. "He'll be somewhere by your buddy. Where'd your black buddy go, devil?"

Ganns didn't move and he didn't answer. He focused on breathing in and breathing out, trying to stay calm, and now he kept his eyes open. She was getting closer. Her voice was starting to crack.

"WHERE DID HE GO?" she screamed at him, waving her arms up in the air. He couldn't see the pistol because she was too close, and it was too high, but he hadn't seen her set it down. She leaned over, the pistol pointed at his head. Her eyes were wide and white. "Where?" she spat, lowering the revolver tip to his nose and pulling back the hammer. "Where is he?"

Ganns thought of Darryl and shifted again.

"We're going to miss them," Sh'Nae said, looking around. They were no longer in along the edges and were now hurrying down the center of the street with Gil at the front. After she'd left, he quickly came up and passed her, and now Sh'Nae was having a tough time keeping up with him.

"I know where they're going, okay? And when. I'm just trying to keep us uninvolved." He was still heading generally toward the direction they'd been heading in, but he'd thrown in a couple of jogs, turning left and right and left and right. It wasn't like he could hide the crowd noises, which they were much closer to now. It might be the right direction. In the dark and strangeness of the city, she wasn't certain.

They headed up the street with Gil checking his wrist before every corner. "We'll come around from the far side, okay? That way the crowd will be looking away from us and toward the house."

"What house?" Sh'Nae asked. She was getting winded.

"1200 block of Saratoga. That's where this is all happened."

"Happened," Sh'Nae repeated. "Right." Though she'd been living it for days, Sh'Nae wasn't used to walking through the past. Everything so far disconcerted her, but not as much as knowing that Darryl (or Robert) was in the middle of it all, and everyone thought Darryl would die. That he *needed* to die. Hopefully Gil and Alex and friends could put a stop to that.

Then there were feet, many feet, coming up from behind. Reflexively, Gil moved into the shadows beside a house while turning his body, and his weapon, toward the noise. He motioned for Sh'Nae to join him.

Several black men jogged together in a tightknit group, rifles in front, all heads-up. Watching them go by, Gil squatted and set the butt of his weapon on the ground. He looked at his wrist again, then motioned for Sh'Nae to take the same position. She shook her head, refusing.

"Things are building up, but we've got a few minutes. There's nothing we can do early."

"Are there more coming?"

"Could be. The whole city's getting rousted." Gil said, laying his gun on the ground beside him. "We had the wrong Robert each time we've been here before, but Alex figured out a way to get the right Robert. You were part of that scheme." He looked up at her. "You volunteered, you know."

"This isn't real," Sh'Nae said. She couldn't think of anything else to say.

"That's how these things are scripted. It's what we do, and you've done a hell of a job."

She stared at him, trying to understand.

"We're on the same side, you and me. You and me and Alex and Ganns. And I'm sorry about Ganns. We all are."

"So that thing with the liver is real?"

"Oh yeah, that's real. It's a chance we all take. You took it. I took it. He took it and lost."

"So Ganns is dead?"

"Right now? I don't know. I know he doesn't make it out of this, but I don't know when he dies either. I liked Ganns. Really."

There were voices rising out of the dark now, hollering and barks. "Darryl's made the house," Gil said. "This is where we change things this time."

"I hope so," Sh'Nae said, her body following through with muscle memory. She'd known since she saw the picture what she wanted to do, but now the moment was perfect. Sh'Nae took one step forward and kicked Gil across his chin. His head snapped sideways, and he lost his grip on his weapon. She grabbed it, then eyed Gil. He fell on his side, so she'd have to roll him to go through his pack. His hip pouch was exposed and, hoping it was ammunition, she unsnapped it and dug out two black cartridges. They matched the one sticking out of the rifle's butt. She took them, shoved one in each rear pocket, and started running toward the noise.

Unlike Gil, she didn't need a device on her arm to tell her where she needed to be. She just followed the voices. There were occasional hollers, but it was mostly a dull roar now. Like many people confused and chatty. She looked back and saw Gil was still lying still on his side, and realized the kick was better than she'd imagined she was capable of. It wouldn't last though, and he'd be after her. As she jogged past the next cross street, she heard the crowd to her right. She turned to find them only a couple blocks away. The crowd was large, perhaps a couple hundred people, and they were all turned and looking toward their right. Some in the crowd hefted rifles or hand tools or sticks, and many were punching at the air. There was one body on the ground and those nearest it were leaned forward, liking down at the man. Then another body fell, and another. Like a wave hit them, a whole quadrant of rioters dropped to the ground, still. The others backed away, but they didn't run. Instead, they grew louder and angrier. Some were throwing their sticks down the street, down where Sh'Nae couldn't see anymore. The crowd was moving like waves in the sea, pushing back and then swelling forward, but there was a line it wouldn't cross, and Sh'Nae could see why.

From the left came the two lead security members, their weapons held at the shoulder and ready. Behind them floated Darryl, straddled by more security. Then came the others at the rear, with one of those being Alex. Sh'Nae couldn't tell from this distance. It appeared they were doing an excellent job of protecting Darryl, but with all the bodies lying on the ground, Sh'Nae didn't understand the cost. The only thing that was clear was that nothing Alex had said had anything to do with what was happening here.

As she watched, Darryl and his escorts passed through a gateway and out of sight. The rioters swelled out again, stepping over the bodies and surrounding the gate.

Sh'Nae stopped. There was no way for her to get to Darryl from this direction. Not unless the weapon she was carrying had hundreds of rounds and she knew how to use it, which she didn't. She chose to go around to the back of the house by staying close to the houses and taking the last cross street. She jogged, holding the weapon up and ready, and keeping her finger near the trigger guard. She hoped there wasn't anything else she'd have to do to fire it.

While the voices were still raging, Sh'Nae broke around the next block only to find some of the rioters had leaked to that edge. There weren't many, maybe twenty, but twenty rioters were plenty to stop her. She saw that the fence surrounding the house was tall, stout, and ran the length of the block. If she could get inside the fence, she could probably get to the house without being seen. She quickly walked across the street, headed around the next block, and came back up. At this end she could only see maybe three of the rioters in the street, and they were less energetic and involved. They paced some, looking back toward the larger crowd, and motioned at each other once. By timing it, Sh'Nae was able to cross the street again and get next to the fence, where she found a gate and slipped inside.

She was at least two houses down, and there were smaller fences between the yards. She could climb over those easy enough. The houses, like several she'd seen on this street, were tall and long. No doubt on the other side, where the rioters were, there would be balconies with iron railings, but on this side, there were broad blank walls with a few open windows. She couldn't see anyone inside any of the houses, but they were probably in there. They were probably hiding. She climbed over the first barrier, a low picket fence with aged wood that cracked when she put her weight on it. She was in a garden now, with greens and peppers and broadleafed plants which were probably some kind of squash. She kept as close to the tall fence as she could, hoping to stay in its shadow, then went to and over the next fence. She kept low, thinking no one wanted strangers in their yard right now.

She found herself on the other side of the gate Darryl had floated through, making the house in front of her the target. She started toward the far corner, the one near the rioters, but stopped short of it. There were figures moving around in the yard, and voices. The sun was low enough that she couldn't place faces, but the one shorter silhouette looked like Alex and the others around her were probably the security team. They were discussing when to go in the house, which Sh'Nae immediately recognized as an indicator that none had yet. She broke out of the shadows, quickly ran for the house's back door, which she found already ajar, and slipped inside.

She was on a back porch, one partially lit by the bright night sky, where she saw a washing tub and wooden racks for drying clothing. There was a doorway to another room, a darker one, and a stairwell going up. Sh'Nae chose the stairwell because she wanted to be able to see, but when she got to the top, she thought twice about it.

The room at the head of the stairs took the entire back half of the second floor, and it was laid out like an apartment. There was a double bed against one wall and a countertop across from it with cupboards above and a long rifle leaning against it. Partial walls in one corner created a small and secluded room not much larger than a closet, and inside it Sh'Nae saw a lone bucket on the floor. There was a doorway leading to the front of the house, but the door was closed. There was another cubby in the corner beside the door, one with a curtain over its opening. The curtain was ajar, and inside Sh'Nae saw clothing stacked on shelves. It was a closet. Beside the closet was a window that would look out over the side yard, down where the others had been arguing. The window was covered by a blanket, and Sh'Nae was just pulling it back to sneak a look when a door downstairs slammed open and voices flooded in. She searched the room, thinking about the closet with the bucket and then beneath the bed, then chose the closest closet to hide. She didn't like the curtain only covering its doorway, but it was slightly wider than the bucket closet and she could probably lift the weapon from inside.

He'd receded into himself when the dead carried him because there weren't any other options. A hundred hands, maybe a thousand hands, made it so.

Since he'd been here, in New Orleans, Darryl felt different. He thought differently. Everything was painted with a clarity he hadn't known on the streets of San Pedro, and for scant moments he'd felt in charge of himself. Even now, clutched by their mottled hands and surrounded by grinning, gray faces, they spoke about the future. Some sang as they passed him along, mixing in a sea of colors and shades and occasional gore. Yes, some of it felt good, but all of it felt like it was too much. Darryl chose to recede.

Moments later the noises around him changed, beginning with anger and shouting, then a series of phut-phut sounds and people crying out. There was screaming, and he waited to be grabbed and thrown, but it never happened. He kept his eyes shut and flowed with it. There was nothing he could do. It was on the dead now. They were chasing their destiny, and he was just their tool. Eventually they arrived there, wherever "there" was, and the hands set him down on the ground softly. The living, mixed together with the dead in a blurry kaleidescope, took a pace back. As he stood there, free, he felt he was still in a fishbowl. He was free only as long as he did as he was told.

They were beside a house and inside a yard, and all the howling and fury was on the other side of a tall fence. A white woman stepped up, a shorter lady with cropped red dish hair and an odd jumpsuit. She held something like a short rifle in one hand. "This is it, Robert," she said.

"This isn't," Darryl replied. He had no idea what she referred to, but he was certain he'd disagree. The reasons, several of them, were clear there in the yard. There were others, each wearing militaristic uniforms, and they were holding others at bay with their short rifles.

"It is," she said. "It's what your whole life has led to. This moment. I know this will sound odd, but you've been here before and it didn't end well. This time I'm here to help you end things differently."

"Help me," Darryl repeated. "Help me?" He looked around. "This doesn't look like help."

"I'm Alex."

"You're no help, Alex. Nor are they." Darryl pointed toward the others who were armed. Alex cocked her head, then shrugged. "Then you can leave," she said. She turned and waved at someone. "Laurie! Open the gate for Darryl. He wants to go." One of the guards stood about twenty feet away beside a gate. She reached over and lifted a latch, pushing the gate out.

Outside, Darryl saw what he'd been hearing, a rabble of armed and angry white people. Laurie stepped partially into the gate and they backed up, but not far. Their sound didn't diminish, either. In fact, they got louder. Darryl didn't move, and he didn't say anything.

"Shut the gate, Laurie." Alex turned to face Darryl again. "Look, I will make sure you don't die, okay? That's my job. The whole thing has to happen, all of it, except you dying. Then we move on, you and I. Understand?"

"Okay. You say I won't die, if you get your way. You're not the only one interested, right?"

"How would you know that?"

"You saw how I got here, right?"

"We saw it, yes. You were carried."

"You know who carried me." It wasn't a question.

"I think so."

"You do. You know. They talked to me all the way here, and they explained how this was all supposed to happen, at least as far as they were concerned. They brought me here, but they're not forcing the rest on me. They expect me to do my duty. That's the way they see it."

"What's your duty? How can you help them?"

"They think I need to die. All of them." He looked around. "None of this is about me."

"No, it's not. It's about the world. The whole world. It's about everyone. It's about existence and the normal."

"For you?" Darryl said. "What about the dead? What about me, Alex? What's normal for me?" He turned and started walking toward the house.

"You have no normal Darryl, because you're the crux of it all. The thing on which all worlds hinge."

"No," he said, still walking. "I'm just a man. A human, like you." He entered the side door and followed the dead leading the way toward the back of the house. It was a boy, a young boy, and he walked with a pronounced limp. Darryl wondered if the limp had anything to do with his death, but decided it didn't matter. The boy moved toward the back of the house and away from the street where the rioters were, and that surprised Darryl. Still, he knew this was the way it had to play out.

They entered a porch and turned up a set of steep stairs, moving slowly, as Darryl was giving the boy time to work his way up. Alex followed him, her steps soft and her breath shallow. *She's calm,* Darryl thought. *Unemotional. Hard, even. Kind of like Sh'Nae.*

Darryl thought about Sh'Nae, and his resolve softened some. She was the one good thing in his life. Without her, he would have probably died in an alley. With her, he got to know someone who listened to him. Someone who cared for him. Even loved him, if that was what love was from her.

At the top of the stairs the boy went straight to the window and stood before it. Darryl walked over, slid the blanket covering it right, and opened the glass. A warm breeze blew in, breaking the humid blanket in the room. Darryl looked out and watched the rioters milling about the street to his right. He leaned out, then leaned back in and looked to Alex. "So, now what?" He noticed that some of the dead were filing into the room from the stairwell.

"You always took out the rifle you had in here and started shooting. Then the rioters shot back. Lots of them. That's what we have to change."

"They," he pointed around the room, "don't want change." Darryl said. Alex looked around, but otherwise didn't react. "How does this work, Alex? How does my living or dying change things."

"We all want a world we can believe in, Robert. For some, that means change. For others, it means keeping things the same."

She was answering *why* and not *how*, but he decided to ignore her. Instead, he said "I'm Darryl."

"I don't know what the dead want from you," Alex continued. "Besides your death."

"I'm Darryl. Just one man named Darryl. My living or dying can't matter this much."

"Not one man. You're you. Specifically, you. Somehow you because you're the axis on which different worlds spin. You're a human holy grail."

"For you, too? What do you want, Alex?"

"I want to do my job. I want to keep you from dying because that's my mission."

"You got me here. Take me out."

"Everything else has to happen. All of it. You just can't die this time."

"Right. If I escape this room, but they catch me outside that gate and hang me, will you care?"

At first Alex didn't answer, but she didn't break his gaze either. Finally, she said "I'm here to fulfill my mission. That is all. I've not been tasked with babysitting you forever."

"I understand. What you want, and what they want," he gestured around the room at the dead standing there, watching him, "is freedom from something. The people in the yard and in the street, they want something, too."

"They want your blood, and they think they'll get it."

Darryl crossed his arms. "Then it's settled. No one gets what they want. If I get shot, fine. If I don't, fine. But no one wins because I'm not starting it. I'm not shooting one person."

"That's not an option, Darryl."

"It's the only option I'm in control of, isn't it? You can make me come up here or the dead can bring me up here. I know they won't let me leave. The people out there, they can shoot me. I can't stop that. The only choice I have is to either start shooting or not start shooting. That's how it's all started. I'm not going to shoot. Not anyone. That's my choice." Darryl leaned against the wall beside the window.

"One way or another." Alex said. She went to the window and pulled the blanket off, throwing it on the floor. Then she leaned out and whistled once. The sound was almost lost in the hullabaloo on the street. Seconds later, a door slammed downstairs, but Darryl didn't move, and he didn't blink.

"I thought this through after last time. I thought all of the options through."

Two of the security guards came in and Alex motioned at them. They both set their weapons down on the floor.

"They're not here to hurt you, Darryl, but if they must, they're going to hold you down and I'm going to show you something. You can choose to look without their help, if you want. Those two can stay right where they're at."

"What do you want me to see?"

"It's on your chest. Can you take your shirt off?" Darryl stared at her.

"I'm staying here and they're staying over there, but only if you take your shirt off and look where I tell you to look. Otherwise, they'll hold you down and I'll cut your shirt off and you'll still look where I'm telling you to look. We're going to end up in the same place in just a few minutes, either way. The path you choose is up to you."

"Okay," Darryl said. He unbuttoned, then sloughed his shirt to the floor.

"You have a couple of scars there, right? On your chest?" Darryl looked down, knowing what she was talking about. There were two, about an inch apart, on the left side of his chest. He didn't answer, but he touched them. His chest was slick with sweat, and he wiped it away with his palm.

"You can pull them open. Like this." She held up one index finger and one thumb, pressed together, then popped them apart. Darryl looked at her and shook his head. "I don't want to use them," she said, pointing at security, "but I will. I need you to see this. Do it yourself and I won't have to." Darryl looked at the security guards, and one, a fellow a little shorter than Darryl but significantly stouter, nodded. He put two fingers together over the scar he could see the easiest, the one nearest the middle of his chest, and he pressed in. When he pulled back, he couldn't feel it, at least not like pain in his chest, but he knew it tore. He looked down to see a hole, one no bigger than one of his fingernails, in his chest. There was no blood. No liquids. Just a hole. He moved his fingers to the other hole and repeated, and it opened as well. He looked up at Alex, waiting.

"Those were the bullet wounds, Darryl. The original bullet wounds you received when you were Robert Charles. The ones that you initially lived through long enough to run away, to leave this house."

"What do you mean long enough?"

"You're good at what you do, you know that? This story has played out before, with multiple Robert Charles, and things are always changing. Lots of different directions, with different people. This time, though, it's really different."

"What do you mean?!"

"Why do you have two holes in you, but you don't bleed? Do you know, Darryl? Or Robert, rather."

"I'm Darryl, and no I don't."

"You've been Darryl for about five years, that's all. Before that, and since the 1860s, you were Robert Charles. You had other names in there, at different times for different reasons, but you were always Robert Charles. You're still Robert Charles today.

"Have you ever heard the story of Eurydice and Orpheus, Robert? She died, but with the help of Orpheus, her love, she was almost able to walk out of Hades. She was almost free. Things didn't go her way at the end, and she had to return to Hades. The story focuses on the misery of Orpheus, but I always think of Eurydice instead. She died, and Orpheus wouldn't let her remain dead. In the name of his own love, he tortured her. I think it fitting that he looked back. I think it's wonderful.

"The reason you don't bleed is because you're already dead. You've been dead since the first time you walked this route as the first Robert Charles back in the first 1900, yet you walk. Every Robert Charles afterward ends up really alive or really dead, but not you. Somehow, you manage to be both. You're the only Robert Charles that's ever done that, and it's what makes you special."

He looked down at one of the holes, but he couldn't bend his neck far enough to see inside. Probing it with the tip of one pinky finger, he spread the hole enough to get his finger in to the first knuckle. Then the skin tightened.

"That's why I see the dead?" he asked. Alex nodded. "We think so. There aren't any experts on this. As far as we know, you're the only one who's ever been on both sides of mortality at once."

"Other people see ghosts. Lots of people see ghosts."

"Not really. They think they do, but people will believe anything."

Robert nodded, probing his wound.

"The way the world is toying with you, it isn't fair. We can stop it now, Robert. We can end this."

He looked up. "How? Are you going to be the one who kills me, then?"

"That won't work, right? If you get shot, and you've always been shot, you'll keep coming back. You'll keep coming back and I'll keep trying to change the ending and neither of us gets any respite. I compared you to Orpheus, but you're more like Sisyphus or Prometheus. By extension, so am I."

"I don't know them."

"It doesn't matter. Guys," Alex motioned to the security people, and they picked up their weapons and aimed them at Darryl. "I'm going to give you an old firearm, Darryl. One with bullets. If you point it at me, or if you point it at them, they will shoot you, but they'll shoot you with non-deadly rounds. It won't end anything. If you point it at yourself, you can take control. You can end this."

"You want me to shoot myself?"

"You're already dead, Robert. You've been dead for a long time, and you've been dead many times. Something has to happen that's different, which means either you don't get shot at all or you shoot yourself. You're not leaving here, you said so yourself. The dead won't let you. Shooting yourself is the only option I can think of. You're the only one who can make this time the last time." She opened her jacket, exposing a holster, and pulled a pistol out of it. Taking it by the barrel, she stepped closer and held it out at arm's length. Robert took it, then looked to security. They had their rifles up at eye level and ready.

"I won't shoot you, and I won't shoot them." He looked at the pistol. "I don't think I'll shoot at all. This isn't for me to end." He thought for a second. "How many times has this happened?"

"I don't know for sure."

"Were you involved every time?"

"Not hardly."

"Who else was?"

"It's not important."

"And the dead? How about the dead? Were they involved before?"

"We can't see them or hear them, Robert. Only you can. But I doubt it, since you are the only Robert Charles who could see them."

"None of the others talked about them before?"

"No."

"The world's filled with the dead, Alex. You know that? Those streets are nearly impossible to move through because they're all crowding in. There's young and old and all shades of people. There's thousands out there, more than that even. Just in this city. How many does that make in the world, all of them waiting for me to do something? But you, you want me to do something different. Why should I side with you?"

"You're not siding with me. You're siding with yourself. That's what I'm trying to tell you."

"No, what you're trying to do is sell me."

"Then it's not going to happen? We're going to keep doing this dance? Now that I know the answer begins with the original Robert Charles, and that's you, I'll take you out of the equation another way. We'll return to the Titor Center together and you can stay on the island for an eternity."

"I don't care." He took the pistol and set it on the floor. "I'm not doing this. I'm not going to do anything."

"Doing nothing is doing something, Robert. I must end this, one way or the other. Come on, guys," she said, motioning to security. "I hate this, Robert. You have no idea how much."

"I know," Sh'Nae said as she stepped out of the closet, her rifle also raised. Security startled, and she took advantage of the surprise with two shots. Both security fell immediately. Sh'Nae looked turned to Alex, tipped the muzzle of the weapon at her, and said "I turned it up with the knob here. All the way up."

Alex looked at Sh'Nae, and then back at Darryl. Darryl put one foot out and stepped on the pistol lying at his feet and slid it back against the wall behind him. Then he took two steps back himself.

"This is a new development, isn't it Alex?" Sh'Nae asked.

"Yes. Yes, it is."

"Ganns was right about not trusting you. Ganns was right all along."

"Ganns doesn't matter now, does he? You still matter, Sh'Nae."

"What about Darryl?"

"It's Robert. You know that. And you also heard that he's already dead. Think about that, Sh'Nae. You just killed two living people and you're aiming to kill a third, all for someone who doesn't exist anymore."

"You don't get the past, do you? Something about your understanding of all these worlds, all these realities, screws up how you see history. It counts, Alex. You can't make it go away. No matter what future you live in when you're eighty, you're going to remember all your pasts, aren't you? Or at least you should." Keeping her hand on the rifle's pistol grip, she reached forward to the dial and turned it back. The rifle clicked twice. "When you come around, we'll be gone."

"I left my guards downstairs for two reasons, Sh'Nae. They're keeping the rioters out, and they're keeping you in. You can't get past them. We have to go through with this, because…" Alex didn't finish. She couldn't finish because Sh'Nae shot her and she toppled forward.

"You didn't know I was here, bitch. Let's go, Darryl," Sh'Nae said. "Pick up the pistol first, okay?"

"Sh'Nae. I missed you, Sh'Nae."

"And I've missed you, Darryl. Pick up the pistol, and let's go." She was already heading for the door to the stairs. But Darryl didn't move.

"They won't let me leave," Darryl said. He had his arms bent so that his wrists were tight to his chest, but he was pointing all about the room with both index fingers. "They keep calling me Robert."

She stepped back behind him, set the rifle down, and pushed against his back. His upper torso flexed forward for a moment, but then it pushed back hard. The back of Darryl's head barely missed her chin, then slammed against her upper chest. She lifted hard, but it wasn't enough. It wasn't even close.

She stepped back, and Darryl bobbled upright like a child's punching clown. She had to figure out how to break Darryl's feet free of the spot he was frozen in without breaking his back. He was looking around, straining his neck to see without moving his feet.

"What do you see, Darryl?"

"There's so many of them. It's packed. The room is packed."

"I don't need details about them, Darryl. Don't look at them. What else do you see? What's the room look like?"

"I can see you sometimes, when you're in front of me and one of them doesn't block you."

Deciding that she might help motivate him, Sh'Nae walked around front.

"I saw you for a second, but you're gone. You're behind a big woman. She's huge. Her skin is sliding off."

"Enough, Darryl." Sh'Nae said, taking two steps forward. "Can you see me now?"

Darryl looked around, then smiled. "Hi, Sh'Nae! I can, a little bit. I missed you."

"You said that already. So, what else can you see? Can you see the doorway that leads out? That's the way I came in and it'll be the way we leave."

"I see the top of it."

"Can you take small steps and work your way toward the doorway?"

"They're holding me. I can barely move at all." She saw his face grimace. "I can't even lift one foot."

"Talk to them, Darryl. Tell them that you have to go." He looked at her, his mouth clenched.

"Talk to them, Darryl."

Darryl searched the room, searching for one of the twenty or thirty dead to talk to. They were there, and he was there, but it wasn't like they were there together. For the most part, excepting those who'd grabbed a hold of him, they weren't paying much attention to him at all. They were chatting with each other, standing and sitting, chatting and smiling.

His legs were getting tired.

Surrounded by them as he was, he found their wounds and garish skin colors only a slight distraction. What kept him watching was their eyes, their faces, their joy. Except for Sh'Nae's worried face, the room was a party proceeding. Darryl shook his head and relaxed his muscles, letting go of the tensions that pulled and pushed against the hands grasping him at all corners. He squared his shoulders and waited, because he suspected this is where the buzz would finally come back, but there wasn't a hint of it. There was nothing portending of it, either, like the tickle at the back of his neck or the dry at the tip of his tongue. It was wholly absent.

There was an old guy standing nearby, one who was half a head taller than Darryl and sported a flat top. Unlike everyone else in the room, he was looking at Darryl. He was smiling.

"Sam?"

"We meet again, little buddy. I thought I was done with this mission, but now I guess not."

"How'd you find me?"

"Everyone on this side knows where you're at, Robert. Many, maybe billions of us, I expect, though most aren't here. We're all watching and waiting for you to do the right thing." Sam's smile was even bigger, and Darryl was glad that he couldn't see lower where the blood stains no doubt dried crusty across the clothing he'd stolen off another corpse less than an hour before he died. Darryl found himself wondering if Sam had met the man he'd stolen the clothing from yet.

"What's the right thing, Sam?"

There was a flicker across Sam's face, a moment when it wasn't smiling, but it was a thoughtful face and one which seemed very at home there. "Let me think," he said. He looked around the room, then scratched at his chin. "I'm thinking I don't know. From what I've heard today, and it's only been today, right?" He winked at Darryl. "What I've heard today is that all of us miss all of you, that we want to be together. Together. That's the whole reason I wanted to meet you in the first place, Sam. I wanted us to all be together, but in the living world. Kind of the same, but kind of different."

"Why is it different?" Darryl started to sit, and while he had hands on his shoulders at first, they let go when he wasn't trying to move away. The dead in front of him parted, breaking apart to allow Sam to get closer. Which he did, sitting cross-legged on the floor across from him. Now Darryl could see all the blood. So much blood, and it still glistened.

"It's different. On your side, regardless where you're from or what you look like, you have to eat, to breathe. You want to love. You search for meaning. I'm no expert about this side, obviously, but we have none of that. We have no goals or aspirations. Why would we? Maybe there's a purpose over here, but I'll be damned if I know what it is."

Darryl didn't answer, knowing that it'd make Sam continue. Which it did.

"The afterlife is what you make of it, I guess. It could be heaven, or it could be hell. It could be nothing. I'm kind of wondering if we're all here, like I am, or if those who strongly believed something else are now doing that something else."

Darryl nodded.

"There's no right answer. I mean, think about it. Some of the people I've seen today have been dead for hundreds of years. Which means the people they're pining for are dead, and the dead go back generations past them. There's no giving them what they want, is there? Why even try?"

Darryl nodded, then froze. Where there'd been dead milling about, talking and backslapping, there was now silence. They stood quietly, staring at Darryl and Sam. For the first time since he'd seen the dead, especially on his trip to New Orleans, it didn't make him uncomfortable. Instead, it gave him a stage. And an opportunity.

He stood up, jostling those around him while thinking of the words he'd used with Alex. Maybe they hadn't been listening to him because he was talking to the living. There was a chance.

"Are you all listening to me this time?" he asked. They didn't move. They didn't answer. "Most of you are. I can see it. Listen closely, please. I'm not shooting. I'm not going to the window. I'm not playing through this the way you want me to. You can stand me up and you can carry me in front of the window, but you cannot make me hold the rifle because you can't pick it up. You can't, and I won't."

Sam looked up at him. "Do you know what that means to you, Darryl? If you come up with a new ending, it'll change everything for you, too."

"Does that mean all this ends this time, Sam? It ends because there aren't any others in both worlds?"

"I don't know. Maybe for you. Probably for you."

"Then it won't matter for the rest of the worlds?"

"It never matters, does it? There'll always be some trying to change things and others keeping them the same. In every world all the time. They might as well be one."

Darryl knew he liked Sam at first, and he liked him still. He decided to repeat himself. "It's the end. I'm not going to the window and I'm not firing. I'm not getting shot and we're not coming together." Darryl turned to the right and toward the door, taking a single step. An old white man stood there, thick of frame and slightly shorter than Darryl. The right side of his body was burned black and no arm hung from the right socket. He stared at Darryl, his eyes rheumy.

"It's over," Darryl said, and he stepped forward. The man fell backward but was caught by someone behind him and stood back up. Darryl took another step forward and the burnt man stepped aside. There was someone young behind him, a girl who probably hadn't made her teens. She was rail thin, almost a skeleton. She stepped aside.

Darryl took three small steps that way, one and wait, looking into the eyes of each of the dead before him. They wouldn't back away until he closed on them, but then they would. He felt hands on his shoulders and hands on his sides, but they were touching him and not grabbing.

He saw Sh'Nae moving across the room, sometimes behind the dead and sometimes through them, and toward the door. She was preparing to lead the way, and he intended to follow.

Background noise from the dead began as he took his steps, and it started in whispers. Darryl knew there was a chance that things weren't going as well behind him as they were in front, but he didn't want to turn around. To turn around was to look at the window and the future they wanted, and he couldn't give them that. It was false hope. He stepped forward again. Then again. Then he heard another noise, a loud bang followed by hammering footsteps. Many hammering footsteps. Two black men burst into the room and past Sh'Nae, not even seeing her.

"Darryl!" Wallace said. The man beside him looked at Darryl, then back at Wallace.

"What about Robert Charles? I thought we were looking for Robert Charles."

"He is Rober…" Wallace started, but there was sliding from across the room, and a voice nearly identical to Darryl's said "I'm Robert Charles. I don't know who this man is." The man picked up the long rifle leaning against the wall. "That was quite a show," he said. He looked at the guards and Alex lying on the floor. "But now you're done. It's my turn."

Darryl could see why people kept calling him Robert, because he was the twin of the guy who rolled out from under the bed. They were the same height, same build, same face, even the same voice. The other guy was stockier and his hair unkempt, but those were the only differences. That was when Darryl also started to realize that the dead were fading. They were there still and just as many in number, but they diminished, their colors thinning like fog burning off beneath the sunlight.

Sh'Nae was up against the wall the door was on, hiding when Wallace and some other man rushed blindly past her. She had her rifle up, but her mouth closed, and Darryl supposed she was waiting for something to happen. Neither of them raised their pistols, but they did take a long look at Alex on the floor.

"You know her, Garrison?" Wallace asked. Garrison shook his head, then ignored her and had started to walk across the room when he looked back and saw Sh'Nae. He started to raise his pistol, but she waved the rifle tip in his direction. "We don't want anything to do with your story, gentlemen. Darryl and I are going to leave now, and you three can carry this forward any way you like. Come on, Darryl." Sh'Nae nodded toward Darryl, then froze.

"What the hell?" Wallace asked. Garrison just stood, his mouth open.

None of them had seen the dead fade the way Darryl had, because they couldn't see the dead in the first place, but now they were seeing it with Darryl himself. He stood frozen as he had when he first saw Robert Charles, his head turned and his mouth barely open, as if he were just about to speak. Whatever was happening wasn't happening quickly. It was like time was slowly brushing him away, gentle flick by gentle flick. Sh'Nae wanted to rush up and grab hold of him, but something told her that it wouldn't matter. Plus, she didn't intend to take the rifle off of any of the men on the other side of the room.

"This doesn't change anything for me," Wallace said. "I wasn't here for him, I came to protect Robert. You," he pointed at Sh'Nae, "can get out on your own."

"I'm not going anywhere," Robert said, reaching over for his rifle. "Get out of here, Wallace. You too, mister. Lady, you vamoose. I picked this fight."

"They're going to kill you, Robert. I've seen it." Wallace tried to walk toward Robert but paused when Robert raised his rifle. "I know," he said, his voice low. "I know. Now get. You have about sixty seconds before I start shooting."

Darryl was about half-faded by now, and though Sh'Nae knew she wasn't going to see him again, she couldn't stand leaving while there was any of him left. On the other hand, the steel in Robert's voice wouldn't brook any disagreement. She lowered the business end of her own rifle and waited. Maybe the delays the other two men were creating would be enough.

"How'd you get in?" she asked. "Weren't there guards downstairs?"

"They're at the fence holding off the white folk. We sneaked in over the far fence, from the other side."

"They won't stay there once he starts shooting. They'll come for her. These," she shook the rifle she held, "are a hell of a lot more effective than those old pistols you're holding. We need her to get out of here alive. You two carry her and I'll go first. They know me."

"You with them?" Garrison asked, already pocketing his pistol. Wallace followed his example.

"Not in a friendly way, no," Sh'Nae said. With flicks of her eye, she kept checking on Darryl. He was nearly gone now, with his lips only an outline and his eyes almost holes. His clothing blended with the surrounding raw wood of the room. "Come on, pick her up and lead the way down the stairs. When we get to the bottom, I'll get beside you and we'll go out with my rifle at her head." While she was talking, she saw Robert standing there, watching them speak with his own lips moving slightly. He was counting to himself.

"We've only got a few seconds left," she said, nodding at Robert, and that kicked Garrison and Wallace into gear. They picked up Alex beneath the arms and started toward the stairs, dragging her feet behind her. Alex took a last look at Darryl's outline, blew him a kiss, and followed.

CHAPTER SEVEN

Year: 1940
Location: Corinth, Mississippi

She was sitting in a rocker when the redheaded lady turned down the path from the road to her front porch. Immediately Sh'Nae knew who it was, because there weren't any short, stocky redheaded white women in this part of Mississippi. There were very few white people at all. She continued to rock and continued to watch. As Alex grew closer, she lifted both of her hands, palms facing Sh'Nae.

"Don't mean a thing." Sh'Nae said. "You're wearing a coat!" Her rifle was inside the doorway, but she wasn't inclined to get up to get it. She couldn't imagine a reason why Alex would be a threat. In answer, Alex opened her coat and spread it wide, proving there was nothing beneath it. When she walked up, she wore a small grin.

"It's been a while," Alex said, and it had. For Sh'Nae it'd been forty years, forty real years. A good part of that was spent in New Orleans, but she'd decided to retire back to the land where she'd been born, back to Mississippi. There were years on Alex's face as well, and her red mop was faded to the point where it looked nearly pink. Sh'Nae found it pretty.

"Sure has. You still working?" She motioned at the other chair on her porch, a harsh wooden upright that, considering the trouble Alex had been, seemed just about right.

"I retired, just a few weeks ago. It's been two decades since I saw you last. I still remember the headache, though. Those guns leave a proper hangover. Thanks, by the way."

"For shooting you? My pleasure."

"No, for dragging my butt out of there before the real Robert started up the fireworks."

"No problem. I figured they'd know how to wake you up and we could shift out of there. It wasn't selflessness."

"Either way, thanks." She took the empty chair on the porch and stared at the overgrown yard she'd just walked through. "This place is beautiful. It's just so green."

"Black, too. Very black. You're not here on business?"

"No, no business. In my line of work there's a word for what I'm doing here. We call it a 'wrap'. It's closure for those cases you never got to close on. We're not allowed to wrap when we're active, but we can after we turn in our papers, as long as we follow some rules."

"You're probably not supposed to shoot people anymore."

"Yeah, that's one of them. How have you been?"

"Okay. It wasn't long after you saw me that I decided to shift to your New Orleans. There wasn't anything back in San Pedro anymore. That life went with Ganns and Darryl."

"Robert."

"He'll always be Darryl to me."

"What happened to him?"

"He faded away."

Alex didn't say anything but kept looking at Sh'Nae.

"And Ganns?" Alex finally asked.

"I never saw Ganns again. I guess he died, too."

"You think he might have shifted instead?"

Sh'Nae shrugged. "It doesn't matter, does it? He wasn't there then, and we can't follow the dead wherever they go. To quote an author who was famous in the time before I knew you, 'sometimes, dead is better.'"

Alex stood and put out a hand, which Sh'Nae took and shook after she stood. "That's it, then. I just wanted to thank you. I'm going to shift now. You won't see me again."

"Fair enough," Alex said. Alex started walking back down the path toward the road but shifted before she got there.

Sh'Nae took her seat and waited several minutes, just to be sure, before she called out "okay, Blue." The cabin's front door cracked open and Ganns stuck his head through the crack. When he saw the porch was clear, he came out and sat on the chair Alex had just left. "I told you she was coming," he said.

"You did. You know why?"

"She's working on something. I suspect it won't be the last time you see her."

"You always suspect something, but this time I think you're right. We won't be able to hide you for long, if you're who she's looking for."

"Yeah, and she can find me. I don't care. I can pop in and out faster than she'll ever be able to and we can play tag forever." He stood up and leaned over, giving Sh'Nae a kiss on the cheek and turning back toward the door to go inside. "By the way, Robert sends his love."

"It's Darryl," Sh'Nae said.

ABOUT THE AUTHOR

Michael Huyck has been in a variety of anthologies, collections, and magazines, both paper and electronic, since the mid-1990s. His credits include: *In Laymon's Terms*, *Into The Darkness*, *A Walk on the Darkside: Visions of Horror*, *Space and Time*, Gothic.net, Horror Garage, and many more. He edited fiction for *Carpe Noctem* and his non-fiction has been placed in publications such as the reference collection Supernatural Fiction Writers and the Stoker award-winning *Jobs In Hell*. Michael Huyck's short story collection, *Of Dark and Yesterday*, is available from Crossroad Press.

Curious about other Crossroad Press books? Stop by our website:
http://crossroadpress.com
We offer quality writing
in digital, audio, and print formats.

Subscribe to our newsletter on the website homepage and receive a
free eBook.

www.ingramcontent.com/pod-product-compliance
Lightning Source LLC
Chambersburg PA
CBHW071134200626
46817CB00018B/2947